9/16

For Lauren Fortune – thank you!

Scholastic Children's Books
An imprint of Scholastic Ltd
Euston House, 24 Eversholt Street, London, NW1 1DB, UK
Registered office: Westfield Road, Southam, Warwickshire, CV47 0RA
SCHOLASTIC and associated logos are trademarks and/or
registered trademarks of Scholastic Inc.

First published in the UK by Scholastic Ltd, 2016

Text copyright © Paula Harrison, 2016
Illustrations copyright © Renée Kurilla, 2016

The right of Paula Harrison and Renée Kurilla to be identified as the
author and illustrator of this work has been asserted by them.

ISBN 978 1407 17058 9

A CIP catalogue record for this book
is available from the British Library.

Printed by CPI Group (UK) Ltd, Croydon, CR0 4YY
Papers used by Scholastic Children's Books are made
from wood grown in sustainable forests.

1 3 5 7 9 10 8 6 4 2

www.scholastic.co.uk

Robyn Silver

THE MIDNIGHT CHIMES

PAULA HARRISON

ILLUSTRATED BY RENÉE KURILLA

■SCHOLASTIC

A Creepy Creature Comes to Visit

can remember desperately wishing my life would get more exciting. We all do, right? Every week's the same: school – homework – brush your teeth – go to bed. It's even worse when you have four brothers and sisters moaning at you and hogging the TV. But if I'd got the chance to pick *how* things would get more exciting, I'd have chosen owning a pool with a water slide or winning a lifetime's supply of free pizza.

I wouldn't have picked seeing freaky things in the middle of the night and discovering a whole creepy world that most people don't know about. Trust me: no one needs excitement like that.

The first time I saw something weird was one

Wednesday at midnight when the clock at Grimdean House woke me up. As it finished striking twelve, I heard growling outside. Drawing back the curtain, I saw a creature with angry eyes and brown spines scratching round our front garden. It gave me this strange shiver that ran right from my shoulders to my feet. The creature was small – less than half my size – but it looked mean, like a goblin crossed with a porcupine.

The odd thing was that when my little sister, Annie, woke up and crept over to the window, she didn't notice it. The creature had spotted us though. It stared back with evil, piercing eyes, before vanishing into a bush. I got the feeling it didn't like us very much but I told myself not to panic. As long as it stayed out there we were fine. Why would a spiny thing want to come inside anyway?

I was standing in the kitchen a couple of days later when the same shiver ran through me. I stared round quickly. Was the creature inside? I didn't want to see it, but believing it was here and *not* being able to see it was worse.

Everything looked normal – the dented kitchen table, the wooden cupboards and the pile of washing-up next to the sink. My sister Sammie was standing by the oven stirring gravy, her wavy hair pinned back with a clip. My elder brother, Ben, was sitting at the table with earphones in. Annie was colouring a picture and my younger brother, Josh, was trying to pinch the crayons from her. Nothing else moved. If there was a creature here, it was pretty well hidden.

I ducked to look under the table. Then I peered behind the door and checked the dark corner beside the washing machine. Nothing.

"Robyn, what are you doing?" Sammie banged the saucepan with her wooden spoon.

"Nothing," I said.

Having so many brothers and sisters basically sucks. What sucks even more is being number three out of the five of us – being smack in the middle, like the meat in a sandwich. The older ones – Sammie and Ben – get to do cool stuff that I'm not allowed to, like go to the teen rollerblading night at the sports centre. The younger ones – Josh and Annie – are totally spoilt.

I just get moaned at by everybody, AND I have to share a room with Annie because we're the two youngest girls (even though I'm eleven and she's six). That's what it's like in the Silver family – everyone talks at once, and if you don't sit down fast enough

3

for dinner most of the food's gone before you've even picked up your knife and fork.

"Robyn!" Sammie rolled her eyes at me. "Get the cutlery out, and the table mats. Hurry up!"

"In a minute." I scanned the kitchen and shivered again. I still couldn't see it. Maybe it was somewhere outside. Maybe I was just cold and my shiver had nothing to do with any creature.

I pulled the drawer open, grabbing a handful of cutlery. Then I opened the cupboard and reached for the mats. Suddenly, something growled. An angry blur of spikes and claws leapt out of the cupboard, and I jerked backwards so fast that masses of knives, forks and spoons flew out of my hand and scattered all over the floor.

The brown spiny thing bared its sharp teeth. It was the same creature I'd seen outside at night, although close up it looked even wilder and spikier. It smelt totally disgusting, like the stink of bad drains. Pouncing on to my left foot, the creature sank its teeth into my bunny slipper, which luckily for me was well-padded with fluff.

I kicked out, shaking the thing off my foot. It crouched on the floor, still growling.

"Robyn!" snapped Sammie. "What are you

doing? You'll wake up Mum. You know she went to bed with a headache."

"What? I couldn't help it! This thing jumped out at me." I looked round for something to use as a weapon. Why weren't they helping me? Did they *want* me to be eaten by a goblin-porcupine? "Er . . . guys! I need some help here!"

"Why?" Ben raised one eyebrow. "Did you see a mouse? There's no need to go crazy. It won't hurt you."

It was my turn to stare. A mouse!

"I want to see the mouse!" Annie said excitedly. "Can you catch it, Robyn, and then I can keep it as a pet?"

"It's not a mouse!" I pointed at the spiny thing which was running up the wall. It dashed across the ceiling and hung upside down, as if its feet were glued there. It was the freakiest thing I'd ever seen.

"I'm sure she was adopted," Sammie said to no one in particular. "I cannot be related to someone so stupid."

"Can't you see it? It's there!" I was still pointing.

Sammie ignored me. Ben, Josh and Annie stared at the ceiling, the same puzzled look on their faces.

"Is it a spider?" Ben said.

A horrible frozen feeling grew inside my

stomach. They really couldn't see it. None of them. What was going on?

The creature growled and a blob of spittle fell from its mouth to the floor. I had to get this weird thing out of here fast.

"What's going on?" Mum came in wearing her dressing gown.

"See! You woke her up," Sammie hissed at me.

"No, I was already awake," Mum smiled peaceably. "I was reading actually."

Sammie shot me a black look. "You *disturbed* her."

Usually I would have glared back, but the creature on the ceiling was distracting me.

"Nothing to worry about. We just had a Robyn-shaped disaster." Ben, who'd started picking up the cutlery, slapped me on the shoulder and nearly sent me flying. It was a family joke, the Robyn-disaster thing. I didn't make *that* much mess. Not really.

"Robyn won't catch the mouse for me." Annie frowned and stuck her thumb in her mouth.

While she wasn't looking, Josh took her last crayon and went to watch TV.

"A mouse?" Mum looked alarmed.

I glanced at the spiny thing – it was still stuck to the ceiling, but at least it wasn't moving any more. What was I supposed to tell them? If they couldn't see it then they'd never believe me. "It's not a mouse," I told her. "I thought I saw something, but it was nothing."

Mum smiled and went to check the pie in the oven. I helped Ben pick up the last of the knives and forks, but then the creature started creeping across the ceiling. I'd have to be quick if I wanted to catch it and get it out of the house. Soon Mum would dish up the pie and the "hordes would descend", as Dad described our mealtimes.

Grabbing the broom from the cupboard under the stairs, I climbed on a chair and swiped at the creature. If I could get it down off the ceiling then maybe I could drive it out the door.

"What are you *doing*?" Sammie said in her best tone of loathing.

Mum turned round. "Robyn, what's the broom for?"

"I'm getting rid of a cobweb." I prodded at the creature. "I'll only be a minute."

The thing's eyes bulged with fury. It bit into the broom handle, making a loud crunching sound. I looked round, certain my family would have heard, but they didn't react.

The creature hurled itself at me, spikes bristling.

I waved the broom wildly and hit it in mid-air. It yowled and spiralled away from me, landing on the table with a *thunk*.

"Robyn, are you kung-fu fighting the cobweb?" Mum asked me.

The spiny thing turned in her direction and scrunched up its body as if getting ready to launch. I jumped from the chair to the table, stumbling to my knees. At least I was between Mum and the creature.

"Hell-oo, I'm home!" The back door swung open and my dad stood there in his blue overalls. He works as a maintenance man for the town council.

The creature scampered across Annie's picture and I dived at it, afraid for my little sister. Its teeth fastened on to my hand. A burning pain shot through my skin and I yelped and dropped the broom. I saw my dad's confused expression but there was no time to explain. I had to get rid of this monster before it hurt someone else.

I grabbed the broom again and swung it like a baseball bat. It smacked into the creature, sending it flying off the table. It gave one final growl and then darted straight past my dad's legs, through the open door and out into the darkness.

Dad didn't even blink.

I jumped off the table, holding my hand to my chest, and slammed the door shut behind it.

"It's welcome to the madhouse, is it?" Dad pulled off his shoes. "Great acrobatics, Robyn."

"Yeah, sorry! Just getting rid of a cobweb." I ran into the hallway before anyone could ask me any more questions.

I leant against the side of the stairs, my hand trembling. A bead of blood was sitting, round and crimson on my skin, so I ran upstairs to wash it off. My hand felt sore but that wasn't the main thing that bothered me.

Something no one else could see had hurt me.

That ruined my last hope – the hope that I was imagining everything; the hope that I'd dreamt the creature up in the middle of the night.

It meant the spiny thing was real.

Tree-maggedon
Strikes our School

That night I heard growling in the front garden again. Two spiny things were clambering through the bushes and snarling by the door. I got into bed and pulled the covers up tight. With the doors locked, I hoped they couldn't get in. I shivered and waited. After a few minutes everything went quiet. Did that mean they'd gone, or were they up to something?

Annie was asleep with her favourite teddy, Mr Huggle, tucked under her chin. Her quilt rose and fell as she breathed. There was an empty packet of sweets on her bedside table which she must have sneaked out of the kitchen cupboard. Sammie thinks she's the pretty one in our family, but really it's Annie. Us Silvers have this gangly look – skinny arms and legs and wavy brown hair that never looks tidy. All except Annie. She has fine golden hair and pink cheeks, and old ladies always coo over her in the street.

I watched her sleeping for a minute and then crept out of bed. I couldn't stand not knowing what the creatures were doing. I went to the window again and pulled back the corner of the curtain. One spiny thing was shuffling away down the street, but where was the other one?

Suddenly, spines scraped against the glass, and black, beady eyes glared at me. I dropped the curtain, my heart skittering like a leaf in the wind. The creature must have walked all the way up the wall to stare in. Maybe it was the same one I'd hit with the broom and now it wanted revenge. The bite mark on my hand throbbed painfully.

A minute ticked by, but it felt like for ever. At last I grabbed the torch off my bedside table and lifted the curtain again. The creature was walking back down the wall. It reached the ground and disappeared into the darkness. I watched the front garden for a while to make sure it had definitely gone. Why did it have to be *me* seeing these things?

Ben was the one that read all the scary horror stories with zombies and stuff.

A few streets away, the Grimdean clock chimed half past the hour.

"Robyn?" Annie said sleepily. "I'm hot. Can we have the window open?"

"No, we can't." I told her. "Now go back to sleep."

I was still thinking about the spiny creatures the next morning on the way to school. I was going to have to tell Aiden about them. We'd been friends for ages – ever since he built a super-fast go-kart and I was the only one who'd dared ride with him. If anyone would understand without teasing me, it was Aiden.

I went round the corner into Ashbrook Street past the maple tree whose leaves were turning red. The wind swooped in, pulling off a handful of leaves and spinning them to the pavement. There was a lot of noise in the playground, but I didn't really take much notice until a fire engine roared up the road with its lights flashing. It stopped at the entrance to our school and one of the firemen climbed down.

"Robyn!" Aiden McGee bounced up to me, the

sun shining on his round face and dark hair. "This is the Best Day Ever!"

"What's going on?" I asked. Aiden didn't usually bounce on a school morning. He usually grumbled. The only time I'd seen him look this excited was when we got to use saws in a design & technology lesson.

"Tree smackdown!" He waved his arm at the school roof. There were three huge trees lying on top of it.

I gaped. The enormous tree trunks had crushed the roof in, and tiles were scattered all over the playground. "Woah! When did that happen?"

"Last night!" Aiden grinned. "This is Tree-mageddon! They'll have to send us home!"

A chant rose in the air, as if every child had thought the same thing at exactly the same moment. "No more school! NO MORE SCHOOL!"

I gazed at the red-brick building that I'd been coming to since I was five. The block for the younger kids, where Annie and Josh had lessons, was on the left with flowers and a rainbow painted on the window. Mum would be walking them up the road right now. To the right was the older kids' block, mostly hidden by a mass of branches and leaves. The trees, which had stood at different corners of the building, couldn't have caused more damage if they'd tried.

"Awesome!" I grinned at Aiden. "It must've been the wind. They'll probably close the place for weeks!"

Mrs Lovell, our headmistress, was talking to a fireman. She was a short, round lady with flat grey hair and a habit of fiddling with her necklace when she was flustered – which she was right now, of course. Kids were jumping and dancing all around her, crazy with excitement and shouting, "NO MORE SCHOOL!"

I pushed my way through the crowd with Aiden behind me. I wanted to hear what was going on.

"We must evacuate the playground," the fireman was telling Mrs Lovell. "More tiles could blow down at any moment."

"But ... the children!" Mrs Lovell twisted her necklace frantically. "What about them?"

"Maybe the council can make alternative arrangements." The fireman straightened his helmet. "This building won't be safe for months. It'll need a whole new roof and there could be a lot of repair work inside too."

"But there's nowhere else for us to go!" said Mrs Lovell. "The town hall isn't big enough and the sports pavilion's being renovated."

"I'm sorry about that, but right now we just have to clear this playground." The fireman held a loudspeaker to his mouth. "Quiet please, everyone. Your headmistress wants to say a few words and then we'll need you to leave the area immediately." He handed the speaker to Mrs Lovell.

"I'm so sorry, children," her voice wobbled. "I have bad news. Because of this awful disaster with the trees, the school will have to—" She broke off as a smart black limousine drew up behind the fire engine and a tall, slim woman slid smoothly out of the driving seat.

Everyone looked round and a whisper ran across the playground. "It's Cryptorum's assistant!"

"What's *she* doing here?" Aiden muttered into my ear.

"I don't know but I have a really bad feeling about it." I watched Miss Smiting cross the playground.

Miss Smiting lived in Grimdean House in the centre of town and worked as an assistant to Mr Cryptorum – a strange old man with wild hair and enormous eyebrows. The mansion was one of the oldest buildings in Wendleton and there were loads of creepy rumours about the place. Some kids said that it was full of bats, and that Cryptorum transformed into one and went flying about at night. I'd also heard that there was a dungeon under the mansion where Cryptorum locked up people he didn't like.

Aiden and I were in the oldest class at Ashbrook School, so we didn't believe that kind of stuff any more, but there was definitely something weird about the place. Mr Cryptorum was hardly ever seen in town, and almost never during daylight. Miss Smiting didn't come out of the mansion much either.

With her sunglasses on and her dark hair fastened into a smooth knot, Miss Smiting seemed like someone out of a movie. She glided along, her skirt sweeping the ground. Cutting through the crowd of kids and parents like a knife through butter, she stopped beside the headmistress. "You are Mrs Lovell, yes?" Her voice had a strange accent. "You are the leader of the school?"

It took Mrs Lovell a moment to get herself together. "Um, yes. That's right."

"I have good newsss." Miss Smiting smiled warmly. "Mr Cryptorum offers you the use of Grimdean House for your ssschool while your building is repaired. You are welcome to bring the children right away."

"I'm sorry!" Mrs Lovell flushed. "Did you say we

could move the school into Grimdean House? Won't that be rather inconvenient for Mr Cryptorum?"

"Not at all. There are plenty of roomsss downstairs that you will use." Miss Smiting said firmly.

"It's a lot of children," put in the fireman. "And a lot of noise."

"But we are the only place in Wendleton that has the room, yes?" Miss Smiting took off her sunglasses and turned her gaze on the fireman and then on Mrs Lovell. "You will bring everyone to Grimdean straight away. It is the perfect solution."

"It *is* the perfect solution," Mrs Lovell echoed.

"Well that's settled then," said the fireman.

Just before Miss Smiting replaced her sunglasses, I caught a glimpse of her eyes – dazzling green with narrow pupils. I sucked in my breath. She glanced at me, her smile bright. "I have ordered a removal lorry for the chairs and desks," she told the headmistress. "You may bring the children to the house and we will make you all very comfortable."

"Wonderful!" Mrs Lovell beamed. "I'll tell them at once." She raised the loudspeaker. "Good news, children! We've been offered the use of Grimdean House while our school is being repaired, so we won't need to close down after all."

The kids groaned. The parents' faces brightened. Soon the teachers had rounded up their classes and a long crocodile of children began marching up the street. I spotted Annie and Josh among them. Miss Smiting glided back to her shiny black limo. The firemen shook their heads as they examined the fallen trees.

"Robyn! Aiden! There you are." Mrs Perez, our class teacher, dumped a tower of books into our arms. "The caretaker's rescued some books and pens from the building. Our class is carrying everything as the younger ones won't manage it."

Even in the middle of all the chaos Mrs Perez still managed to look all neat and organized with her smooth bob and gold-rimmed glasses. She zipped round, piling stuff on to everyone, before leading us up the street. Aiden and I were at the back of the line, mainly because I kept dropping my books and had to stop to pick them up.

"Hey!" Aiden paused just before we turned the corner. "Did you think it was windy last night?"

"No, why?"

"Because those trees have stood next to the playground for years. Wouldn't it have taken a big storm to knock them down? There wasn't anything like that."

I shrugged. Aiden always had to find reasons for things. Sometimes things just happened the way they happened. "Maybe their roots were weak or something."

"I think it's weird that they all managed to hit the school roof. They were at different corners of the building. Why didn't one of them hit the fence or the teachers' car park?"

"I guess... But at least we get a chance to see inside Grimdean House and work out whether Cryptorum really does turn into a bat."

"Mmm." Aiden was still staring back at the school.

I glanced at the roof with its gaping holes and the three tree trunks lying against the building. It did seem a bit strange but I pushed that thought out of my mind. My arms were starting to ache from carrying all the books. "C'mon! Perez has nearly got to the next corner."

Mrs Perez was frowning at us, so we tried to stay with the rest of the class after that. Everyone was still moaning about not getting time off school. Douggie was complaining the loudest. "But where are we going to have PE, miss? And where's the lunch hall gonna be? And will we have the same things to eat?"

Mrs Perez was obviously trying not to roll her

eyes. "I don't know, Douggie. This all just happened a few minutes ago. I expect we'll have to be patient over the next few days while things are worked out."

"Here, miss, shall I take those?" Hector took a few books from the teacher's arms. He was the tallest kid in our class and always acted like class Superman.

"Thank you, Hector. That's very kind. Now hurry up, everyone." Mrs Perez turned down Demus Street. "We're nearly there."

We passed the turn for the town square. The grocer, the shoe shop, and that little place that sold all the shiny stones and pots of herbs were all opening their shutters and putting signs out front.

Halfway down the street on the left was Grimdean House, sitting in the middle of a row of ordinary houses. It was a big, grey monster of a building surrounded by spiky black railings and topped by a pointed tower with slit-like windows. Near the top of the tower was a huge oval-shaped clock with a face of polished gold. The clock hadn't worked for years, but a week ago a workman had been spotted climbing a ladder to reach it and by the end of that day the clock was running again. Mum had told us not everyone liked it because the chimes were so loud. Actually it had woken me up a couple of times over the last few nights.

The front steps of the mansion were swarming with little kids and the teachers were trying to herd them all inside. I glanced up at the clock. There were two dark patches just above the centre which made me think of eyes. I blinked and looked again. They were only patches of dirt. Just because the whole week had been weird didn't mean I had to freak out over nothing.

Bong! The clock began to chime nine o'clock. The deep sound vibrated right down to my toes.

"Robyn, catch up please!" Mrs Perez called.

"Yes, miss!" I glanced up one more time as I followed everyone inside. I was sure I saw a bat gliding over the grey stone tower.

Our Maths Lesson is Haunted

Grimdean House was just as freaky inside as I'd imagined. There was a big arched doorway with strange marks carved into the wooden frame. The entrance hall was huge and dimly lit. Mirrors of different shapes and sizes hung on the walls between candles in black iron holders. At the far end, a massive wooden chest with a rusty padlock stood at the foot of a wide staircase.

"Sssilence!" Miss Smiting's voice cut through the chatter. She stood a few steps up the staircase holding a large bunch of keys in her hand. I wondered how she could see properly in the dim light with her sunglasses on. "Let me direct you to your new classrooms," she began. "The infants will be in the ballroom."

I smirked at Aiden. A ballroom! Who actually has a ballroom in their house, like it's a castle or something?

"Tables and chairs will be brought along to your room shortly." Miss Smiting smiled down at the smallest children. "The older onesss will be in the blue room, the red room and the drawing room. Part of the back lawn will be roped off as a playground but you must keep away from the barn—"

"Junella!" roared a deep voice. A pair of legs came into view at the top of the stairs, dressed in pyjamas, a green velvet dressing gown, and brown slippers. A ripple of laughter ran round the entrance hall then stopped quickly as the rest of the man appeared. Bristling eyebrows jutted out above Cryptorum's deep brown eyes and craggy nose. Grey hair flowed down to his neck like a wild, wintery sea.

"Junella, what is the meaning of this?" he snapped at Miss Smiting. Then he jabbed his gnarled finger towards a little boy. "Get your face OFF my mirror!"

The boy, who'd been pressing his nose against a long rectangular mirror, jerked back from the glass and burst into tears.

"Really, Erasmusss," said Miss Smiting, completely

calm. "This is hardly the way to welcome people to your home."

"Why would I welcome people to my home?" He clumped down the steps until he was level with her. "What on earth are they doing here? Of all the crazy, rattle-brained ideas you've had, this has to be the worst. I can't have children poking around my stuff!"

Mrs Lovell hurried forward, twisting her necklace nervously. "Good morning! I'm the headmistress. I understood you'd offered us the use of your house in our hour of need, but if that's not the case then we'll leave." She blinked rapidly. "And we're very sorry to have bothered you."

I nudged Aiden and whispered, "Bet you five pounds that Lovell starts crying."

"Done!" he whispered back.

"The school roof is damaged, Erasmus, and they have nowhere else to go," said Miss Smiting. "We did discuss thisss before."

"Discuss! Is that what you call it? I agreed to the clock being mended but this is a child invasion." Cryptorum's dark eyes scanned the entrance hall as if he was looking at every single child. I shivered as his gaze brushed past me. "If we absolutely *have* to let them in then they must keep out of my way.

They're not allowed anywhere near my private study, or the barn, or the tower, or the library. In fact they'd better stay out of the whole of the upstairs."

"I'll ssee to it." Miss Smiting smiled. "There's no need for you to worry."

"And I want everyone who comes here thoroughly checked," Mr Cryptorum growled. "No dodgy people are allowed past the front door, and that includes parents!" He stomped back upstairs and the entrance hall was silent for a moment, except for the little boy who was still crying.

Miss Smiting glided over to him and ruffled his hair. "Take no notice! Mr Cryptorum is simply grumpy from being woken early. He often stays up very late indeed." She clapped her hands. "Infantss! Follow me to your new classroom."

The place was like a crazy ant's nest for the rest of the morning, full of lost kids and annoyed teachers. The removal lorry arrived with the chairs and desks, and as we were the oldest kids, we had to carry them inside. Miss Smiting glided about hanging wooden signs on the doors that read KEEP OUT in big black letters. Every time she stuck another one on a door it made me desperate to look inside. The biggest KEEP OUT sign hung on a chain across the stairway. Obviously going upstairs was forbidden.

After carrying a few chairs, me and Aiden perched on a desk in the entrance hall for a rest. The clock on the tower struck eleven o'clock.

"This is hard work," I said. "They should pay us for doing all this."

"The fact is people hardly ever pay children even when they're doing as much work as adults," Aiden said.

"Well, they should!" The clock stopped chiming and suddenly it was really quiet. "This has to be the creepiest place I've ever seen. Seriously! No wonder there are all those rumours." I remembered that with all the excitement I still hadn't told Aiden about the spiny creature. "Hey! Talking of creepy – you'll never believe what happened yesterday—"

"Robyn!" Hector marched in and picked up a stack of chairs. "Mrs Perez is waiting for that desk."

I grimaced at his disappearing back. "He really thinks he's in charge, doesn't he? Mrs Lovell had better watch out because he'll take over the whole school."

"We should go." Aiden yawned and slid down from the desk. Behind him, there was a sudden movement in the mirror. To my horror, a grey face swam towards the glass like a fish coming to the surface of a pond.

I glanced round. No one was behind me. "Did you see that?"

"See what?"

"That thing in the mirror – that face." I jerked my head at the gilt-edged mirror.

Aiden looked into the glass before grinning at me. "Can't see a thing, but an old place like this is bound to be haunted, right?"

I hesitated. I'd been ready to tell Aiden about the weird creature in our kitchen before Hector had come in. But what if I was seeing all this stuff because something was wrong with me?

Aiden knocked on the mirror. "Looks like the ghost is gone!"

I peered in the glass. Aiden was right – there was nothing there. I was sure I'd seen something though. "I don't know why Mr Cryptorum needs so many mirrors anyway. Doesn't look like he spends much time on beauty tips."

"You don't know that," Aiden quipped. "It probably takes a lot of time and effort to make his eyebrows that scary." He picked up one side of the desk and I took the other.

I risked one more look in the mirror as we carried the desk through the hallway, but there was still nothing there.

After that, I really started noticing all the mirrors. They were literally everywhere – in the ballroom where the little kids were and the drawing room which was now our classroom. Every corridor had them too. Maybe Mr Cryptorum collected them.

When me and Aiden brought the desk to Mrs Perez she made us sit down at it and join in the maths lesson. There was no way I could concentrate on fractions after so much had happened. I stared around the room. The leather sofas had been pushed to one side to make space for our desks. There was a cabinet in the corner with rows of china teapots inside. Next to it was a tall cupboard with a key in the lock. And of course there were mirrors – I counted seven of them.

I put my hand up. "Miss, don't you think it's weird that Mr Cryptorum has so many mirrors in his house?"

Mrs Perez frowned deeply. "No, that is not the answer to 'what fractions are equivalent to one quarter', Robyn. Please make sure you're paying attention. Just because this isn't our normal classroom doesn't mean we can let our standards slip. We could be here for weeks, maybe months, so we can't daydream the time away."

Hector raised his hand. "It's two-eighths, miss."

"That's correct, Hector, well done," Mrs Perez smiled.

From the desk in front Sally-Anne threw me a pitying look.

I couldn't help staring around some more though. I tried to imagine what it would feel like to live here with all these enormous rooms and old furniture. I twisted in my chair a bit so I could look at the big painting above the fireplace. That looked really old too. It was a picture of a man and a woman in posh clothes standing in this room – the drawing room. The man had a straw hat and looked a bit like Mr Cryptorum. The woman was wearing a long flowery dress and – my breath caught in my throat – there was something funny about her eyes...

"Robyn Silver!"

I almost jumped out of my chair. "Yes, miss."

"Please give out the textbooks," said Mrs Perez. "Quick as you can. We don't have long till lunch."

I stumbled to my feet and handed out the books, but I kept glancing back at the picture. A shiver ran through me. The eyes of the woman in the painting seemed to be watching me – following me round the room. Mrs Perez sighed as I dropped a load of books on the floor and, as I scooped them up, I could still feel the woman's eyes on me. This was stupid. Paintings couldn't watch people!

I sat down and tried to concentrate on the fractions. Halves, quarters and thirds... Was the woman watching me now? I tried to nudge Aiden but he was leaning really close to his book, his lips moving as he read the next question. Aiden is dyslexic, so reading things takes him longer than me, but give him tools and wood and wire and he can make just about anything.

I glanced at the picture again. From deep below the house came a long moaning sound. It was like something in pain. It grew louder, making the glass in the cabinet door rattle.

"What was *that*?" I said.

Mrs Perez came over. "What's the matter now, Robyn? Are you stuck?"

"No, it's just ... that noise was horrible." I shivered.

Mrs Perez sighed. "What noise, Robyn? The room was quiet until you started talking. Now get on with your work, please."

Sally-Anne sniggered at the desk in front. I fell silent and pretended to do the sums but my mind was spinning. I'd seen things no one else could see. Was I hearing things other people couldn't hear now too?

At the end of the lesson I dashed over to the fireplace, determined to look at the painting. As I got close, there was a flicker of movement in the woman's eyes and a sharp *click*. Then the eyes were still – just like any other part of the painting.

Aiden followed me. "What are you doing? First you stare at the mirrors, now it's the paintings."

"Did you see that?" I demanded.

"See what? What are you talking about?"

"Oh, never mind!" Suddenly I felt like my head was going to burst. I had to get out of this room – out of this horrible house.

"I don't know what you saw." Aiden lowered his voice. "But I did hear that groaning sound. It came from somewhere beneath us."

A wave of relief washed through me. "You heard it? I thought it was just me." I opened my mouth to ask him if he'd ever seen the spiny goblin things too.

"Robyn and Aiden." Mrs Perez cut in. "You obviously haven't noticed but everyone else has gone to lunch. Hurry along now."

A faint scratching began inside the cupboard behind Mrs Perez. The cupboard door opened a crack. I froze. What was in there? Was it another weird creature?

Slowly and carefully, four long, pale fingers slid through the thin gap and wrapped themselves round the edge of the cupboard door. My stomach dropped. There was no skin on those fingers. There was nothing but bones.

I glanced at Aiden. The look of horror in his eyes told me he could see them too. The fingers tightened on the door, making a sharp cracking sound. Mrs Perez was still gazing at me and Aiden as if everything was totally normal. She actually looked a bit impatient, as if we were wasting her time.

I didn't know what was in the cupboard and I didn't want to find out. Bounding forwards, I slammed the door shut, nearly crunching the bony fingers. My heart pounding, I fumbled with the key in the lock.

"Is it really necessary to leap at the furniture like that?" Mrs Perez began.

"I just want to help keep things tidy, miss," I gabbled. "And maybe you should come with us now. . ."

"To show us where to get lunch," Aiden added quickly. "Because we can't remember."

"All right then." Mrs Perez straightened the

pile of textbooks on her desk. "I do hope you two are going to be sensible while the school is here at Grimdean. It seems like a lovely house full of beautiful things and it's very kind of Mr Cryptorum to give us a safe place to learn. Don't you think this is a wonderful place to have a school?"

I sprang back as something thumped the inside of the cupboard. "Yes, miss. It's . . . great!"

Annie Makes
a Wish

e ate lunch in the Grimdean dining room under the crystal chandeliers. Paintings of more posh-looking people stared down at us from the walls and I wondered what they'd think if they were really here. I guess a hundred kids eating lunch isn't too pretty.

"That thing in the cupboard," whispered Aiden as we sat down with our burgers and chips, "do you think it was a fake skeleton that someone put there for a joke?"

I shook my head. "I think it was real."

"No way! How can something like that be real? It must be a prank. Someone must have tied string to it to make it move. . ."

I rubbed the cut on my hand where the spiny creature had bitten me. I wanted to believe it was a prank but I had a horrible feeling I'd just be ignoring the truth.

Aiden munched a chip thoughtfully. "If you think about it we only saw a few fingers – probably plastic ones, so—"

I nudged him as Sally-Anne sat down opposite. She was one of the worst earwiggers in the whole of Ashbrook School, always listening in to other people's conversations. She also made stuff up if she decided what she'd heard wasn't interesting enough. Her aunt was a dinner lady, which was how Sally-Anne seemed to find out loads of things.

"Guess what? Paggley's REALLY angry and says he won't cook here if he's treated this way." Sally-Anne widened her eyes like she always did when delivering gossip. Paggley was our school cook and everyone knew he had a short temper.

"Why?" I knew she was probably making it up but at least it took my mind off those bony fingers. I was starting to feel a bit less shaky.

"Paggley's annoyed that he can't store boxes of food in the basement," Sally-Anne said. "He reckons this place must have a large cellar – all big old houses do – but Cryptorum won't even let Paggley see the basement, let alone use it. And my aunt says Cryptorum has private rooms in the north wing, and the only one allowed in is Miss Smiting."

I rolled my eyes. "Well, it's his house! Having private rooms isn't exactly gossip of the century is it?"

"Oh yeah, Miss Smarty-pants?" Sally-Anne sniffed. "It probably means he's got loads of expensive stuff in there. My aunt says his parents were rich. I bet he's got masses of gold and jewels!"

"Of course they were rich if they owned this huge place." Aiden took more chips. "If I were rich I'd spend it on a massive workshop filled with tools where I could make whatever I wanted."

"I'd buy a house where I could have my own bedroom," I said, looking gloomily at Annie and the other six-year-olds across the hall. She and her friends were pulling faces in the nearest mirror. Sally-Anne sniggered at this, which made me sorry I hadn't let the monster with the bony fingers out of the cupboard and set it on her. Aiden and me finished our lunch and then headed outside.

At the back of Grimdean House, pale marble steps led down to a massive lawn ten times bigger than our school field. Part of it was roped off to be our new playground and a bunch of kids were yelling and running up and down on the grass. To the left, a square of tall hedges divided off part of the garden. To the right stood a wooden barn with a row of holes just below the jutting-out roof. A girl with brown plaits was trying to sneak up to the barn, but an old man in a cap and gardening gloves stopped her.

Me and Aiden sat down on the steps. I knew we were both thinking about the bony fingers in the cupboard. I had to explain to him about the creature I'd seen last night. "I have to tell you something. It might sound a bit weird. Actually it'll sound worse than weird – on a freakiness scale of one to ten this is like one thousand, nine hundred and eighty."

"Did you cut your sister's hair while she was asleep again?" Aiden looked at me curiously. He often found it strange how much I fought with my family, probably because it was just him and his mum at home.

"No, it's not about Sammie. Anyway, I was much younger when I did that." I broke off as a dark speck rose from the barn roof. Suddenly more black specks poured out of the barn, flapping into the air on leathery wings. They circled the garden a few times, causing massive excitement among all the little kids. "I don't believe it! Cryptorum really does have a house full of bats!"

"A barn full of bats," Aiden corrected me. "Listen, I need to talk to you too. You know the thing in the cupboard back there?"

I thought I knew what he wanted to say. "You've met something like that before but no one else could see it – until now, anyway."

Aiden stared at me. "So you've been seeing things too?"

"Yeah. This spiny thing came into my garden last week." I grinned – not because I liked talking about the spiny creatures, but because I was just SO GLAD that Aiden could see stuff too. It meant I definitely wasn't going mad and . . . well, Aiden had been my friend since for ever.

"Why can't other people see this stuff?" Aiden jumped up and paced along the marble steps. "It's been driving me mad. I first saw something on Saturday night – like you said, a creature with spikes all over it. I thought my mum was joking when she said she couldn't see it, but she wasn't. Now we've spotted a skeleton hand!"

"One of the spiny things bit me." I showed him the mark on my hand. "Maybe we can detect freakiness better than other people – it would explain why everyone else likes Hector." I stopped talking as Mrs Perez walked past. "We should go back. I'd rather fight the thing while there's no one else in the room."

"Not a good idea." Aiden told me. "Think about it! The deadly skeleton tried to come out of the cupboard and you slammed its fingers in the door. Now it'll be really mad!"

"C'mon, we have to! What if someone unlocks the cupboard? What if Mrs Perez decides she wants to store her books in there? The creature could get out and attack everyone, and the little kids are only just down the corridor."

Aiden sighed. "All right! I know I'm gonna regret this."

We sneaked back to the drawing room, Aiden grabbing the poker from the fireplace. The eyes of the woman in the painting were still following me. I looked round for something to fight with but all I found was Mrs Perez's rolled-up umbrella. It would have to do. "Just hit it as soon as I unlock the door," I said. "Don't give it time to do anything."

"Got it." Aiden moved towards the cupboard with the poker raised.

Fingers shaking, I turned the key in the lock.

Nothing happened. I tugged the door open, ready to smack the bony thing with the umbrella.

The door swung on its hinges. There was nothing but empty space inside.

"Maybe we scared it so much that it ran away," I said.

"I doubt it. Anyway you locked the door, so how did it get free?" Aiden stared into the bare cupboard. I could see his brain working, like in a cartoon where you get those cogs turning inside someone's head and then a thought cloud hangs above them in the air. He was right about the creature though – there was no way something that creepy had been scared by Aiden and me.

At dinner that night, Mum and Dad asked a million questions about Grimdean House.

"Cryptorum invited the school to move in pretty fast," my dad said. "I don't think anyone except him and his assistant have been inside that house for years."

"It was really Miss Smiting that organized it," I told him. "I think it was her idea." That got me thinking. Why *had* Miss Smiting wanted Ashbrook School to move in when Mr Cryptorum hated the plan so much?

"I think it's a lovely way to make use of all those empty rooms," Mum said as she dished out the stew. "Erasmus Cryptorum can't possibly use all that space on his own. The mansion was built for his grandfather who got rich from the department store he owned in Main Square. He handed the business on to his son, Erasmus's father. I guess Erasmus was supposed to take it on after that but he never did."

"He went off round the world," my dad said. "Must be nice to be rich! I don't think he's ever done a day of work in his life."

"Well, at least now he's doing something good for the town," Mum said. "I haven't seen him for months – hidden away inside that big old mansion. Josh! Don't chew with your mouth open."

"He should do something else that's nice for this town and get rid of that clock on the outside of his house," Dad grumbled. "It's the first time he's had it fixed in forty years, so the newspaper says, and if you ask me it's a shame he bothered. The chiming nearly broke my eardrums when I was working near Demus Street the other day. It's not even a cheerful sound!"

"Yes, it is a bit loud," Mum agreed. "Eat those carrots up, Annie. There'll be no ice cream if you don't!"

I pictured the huge golden clock stuck to the Grimdean tower. I was going to have to live with the noise every day at school now.

Sammie eyed me mockingly. "So you're stuck in Grimdean House. I bet you cried when Lovell said they weren't closing the school." She turned to Mum. "My gym coach says I'm in the team that's going to regionals. She reckons my floor routine's the best out of everyone's."

"Brilliant, honey!" Mum said. "You're doing so well. And after that special merit you got for your geography project too."

I gave Sammie a dead-eye stare. Just because she goes to high school she thinks she's so mature.

I had a strange dream that night. I was following one of the spiny creatures, and it led me all the way through town to Grimdean House. Then the creature disappeared. Cryptorum opened the front door, turned into a bat, and flew away.

I woke up, my heart racing. My watch showed it was quarter to midnight but I didn't feel sleepy at all. I threw off my covers and went to the window. Circles of light from the street lamps patterned the road below. I shivered. That's how I knew one of the spiny creatures was hiding somewhere. It shuffled out of the shadows, spikes bristling, just like it had in my nightmare.

Why had I dreamt about it leading me to Grimdean House? Why did Mr Cryptorum have a barn full of bats in his back garden? The stories about him couldn't be true, could they? That would be crazy.

"Robyn?" Annie said squeakily.

I dropped the curtain, forgetting for a second that she wouldn't be able to see the spiny thing anyway. "Go back to sleep, Annie."

"I can't." She sat up and hugged her knees. "I had a bad dream. It was really scary."

I shivered again. I suddenly wondered if there was some freaky creature in the room. I switched on the lamp and started checking under the beds and behind the cupboards but there was nothing there.

"What are you doing?" Annie said in a small voice.

"Nothing! Just checking for cobwebs." I sat down on Annie's bed and put my arm round her. "Don't worry, it was just a dream. It's gone now and you're fine."

I wanted to believe my own words but what if something managed to get in? My stomach churned. How could Annie keep away from things she couldn't even see?

Annie picked up her teddy and held him tight. "You have a sad face."

I stuck my tongue out and crossed my eyes, making her giggle.

"I *wish* you'd read me a book again," she said. "I liked it when you used to read to me."

"Um. . ." I stared at her. As she was talking, a bright round bubble had floated from her lips and sailed into the air. It had a golden sheen all around it and a picture of a book inside.

For a second, I couldn't speak. I touched the bubble with the tip of my finger. It didn't pop and it felt warm.

"What are you doing?" Annie put her thumb in the corner of her mouth. She couldn't see it. That was obvious.

I glanced again at the bubble. The tiny picture of a book had a unicorn on the cover. "Um, do you want me to read you that story with the unicorn?"

She beamed. "Yes! *Unicorn Goes to School.*" Bouncing off the bed, she went to the bookcase, fetched the book and plonked it on my lap. A white unicorn with a silver horn was galloping across the cover.

The book matched the picture in the bubble perfectly, but how had she made it happen? I thought of what she'd said. *I wish you'd read me a book again.* An idea sparked in my head. "What else do you wish for, Annie?"

She wouldn't tell me until I'd read the story, so I did and then asked her again. "So if you could have any wish, what would it be?"

She smiled like we were playing a game. "I wish I had my own unicorn."

Another shiny bubble, with a confused-looking unicorn inside it, popped out of her mouth and floated up to the ceiling to join the other one.

Her eyes lit up as she had another thought. "Sometimes I wish I *was* a unicorn."

Another bubble popped out. I stifled a giggle because this time there was a unicorn inside with Annie's face and a silvery horn stuck on her forehead. She did look funny.

So that was it – I'd cracked the puzzle. The bubble things were wishes and I could now see them just like I could see the weird creatures. It probably wasn't just Annie's wishes. Maybe I could see everybody's.

"OK, my turn," I said. "I wish I had a whole mountain of chocolate brownies." A soft bubble popped out of my mouth filled with an image of a brownie mountain. It drifted across the room and got stuck in the folds of the curtain.

My talk of food got Annie started on a whole new batch of wishes and soon there were bubbles with pictures of cakes and sweets inside joining the unicorns just beneath the ceiling. She made ten wishes about lollipops, inventing giant ones and rainbow ones and ones that never ran out. She loved lollipops so much.

I had to add a few wishes about chocolate chip cookies, because, yum! Annie's wishes were a lot brighter than mine though. However hard I wished her bubbles always came out much shinier and they bobbed about a lot more and sparkled.

After a while some of the bubbles popped until there were only a few left. One of the ones left behind was Annie's first wish – the unicorn book. Not far away, the Grimdean clock began striking twelve.

I tucked Annie in and turned the lamp off before going back to bed. Once my eyes got used to the dark I could see the last few wishes gleaming faintly as they turned in the air. It was strange to see them but also kind of comforting. I knew the creatures might still be there, outside the window, but in here we had our wishes. Something nice in this new freaky world of mine.

We Find Out What's Hidden in the Grimdean Dungeon

couldn't wait to talk to Aiden about the wish bubbles the following day. At Grimdean House, parents with little kids were waving their children goodbye. Miss Smiting stood by the entrance, keeping a close eye on who went inside.

Aiden was waiting for me on the steps. He pulled me to the side. "I was thinking . . . maybe everyone's been hypnotized, except it didn't work on us and *that's* why we're the only ones who can see these creatures." He kicked the step thoughtfully. "It'd be hard to hypnotize the whole town though. So maybe it was something that everyone ate. Or something that we ate. Or—"

"Hey, I have to show you something." I said.

"And the trees falling down on our school – that makes no sense either!" he continued. "I'm sure they didn't fall down by themselves."

I wasn't interested in the trees. "Aiden! You have to see this!" I took a deep breath. "I wish I had a million pounds. I wish I lived in a giant strawberry cake. I wish I had super speed."

Aiden's mouth dropped open as the wish bubbles floated into the air. "What is THAT?"

"They're wishes! They're cool, aren't they?" I grinned. "I discovered them last night. I *wish* I could make them all day." Another wish bubble popped out of my mouth; like the others, it burst in seconds.

"Hi, Aiden!" A little boy galloped up the steps and ran inside.

"Hi, Finlay," Aiden called back, before muttering, "That's my next-door neighbour's kid. He keeps on wanting to help when I'm working on stuff in the garage."

"Annie wants to help me all the time," I said. "It never goes very well."

The clock on the tower started chiming, telling us it was time to go in. When we got to class we tried out some more wishes and sent them drifting across the classroom. My wish that the lesson would end popped right on Mrs Perez's forehead.

"I wonder why some of them pop right away and other ones don't," Aiden whispered. "What was that one?" He jerked his head at an orange-red bubble bumping against the window. No matter how many times it hit the glass, it still didn't burst.

"I wished that it was pizza for lunch," I sighed. "But from the smell, I think it's probably shepherd's pie again."

The wishing was fun for a while but then the horrible moaning noise started up again. I tried to concentrate on what Mrs Perez was saying but the sound sent icy prickles down my neck.

By lunchtime, Aiden looked grim and my head was aching.

"What's wrong with you?" Sally-Anne combed her hair in front of one of the gazillion mirrors as we lined up for lunch. "You keep staring at everything."

Just then a grey face with mean-looking eyes zoomed to the surface of the mirror, its mouth open in a snarl. I tried not to gasp.

"What?" Sally-Anne stared at her reflection. "Do I have something on my face?"

"No, it's nothing!" When she'd moved on I pulled Aiden aside. "We have to find out what's going on. I've got to know, even if it means meeting the thing with the bony fingers again!"

"That groaning is coming from below," Aiden said. "We need to find the basement."

We dodged round dinner ladies and teachers as we hunted for a door marked BASEMENT or some stairs leading down. In the ballroom we nearly got caught by Miss Rawlings, Annie's teacher, and had to dive under a cabinet before she saw us.

When she'd gone I crawled out again and caught a flicker in the eyes of a nearby painting. "Did you see that?" I muttered. "I think the painting in here is watching us too."

Aiden jerked his head to the right. I went the other way and we tried to sneak up on the painting from opposite directions. The weird eyes belonged to a little painted girl with an umbrella. As I got close, the eyes moved and I heard a sudden click. "That was creepy. It did that before."

"It's like a different set of eyes snapped into place." Aiden peered at the canvas and started knocking on the wall beside it. "Hear that? The walls are hollow."

"You're kidding me!" My stomach turned over.

Aiden moved along, still tapping the wall. "There could be a room behind here – maybe even a passageway."

"Then there'll be a way in somewhere." I ran my hand along the wall until I got to a dusty old tapestry of Wendleton in the olden days. I lifted it to find a door set into the plaster with a sunken latch.

"Look at this!" I held back the tapestry. "This is our way in."

Outside, the whistle blew for the end of lunchtime. A wave of noise surged towards us as a hundred children ran back into the building.

"There's no time," Aiden said. "We'll have to wait till tomorrow."

"No way!" I pressed the latch frantically. "I can't wait that long." The latch clicked and the door swung open. A narrow, dark corridor lay on the other side.

"Robyn, we can't! We don't know what's down there and that groaning isn't exactly a good sign. Anyway, if we disappear Perez will have us in detention for a month."

"I wanna know what's going on! Come on, we need to get inside before anyone comes." I stepped in and the floorboards creaked. It was too dark to see very far.

The pounding of kids' feet grew louder and I leant out and pulled Aiden inside. Then I yanked the door shut behind us. At once all the noise from outside became muffled. I put my hand on the wall to stop myself falling over. It was pitch black with the door shut and I couldn't see a thing.

A light bulb flicked on. Aiden was beside me, his hand on the switch. "This is crazy! Now we can't get out until everyone goes home."

I hadn't really thought about that when I'd pulled him in. "You don't know that. Maybe there's another door."

"Knowing our luck there won't be!"

The voices of the little kids were really close now and I could hear Annie's among them. Creeping along the passage, I found a little round knob on the wall just above my forehead. When I touched it, a small rectangle of wood slid sideways and two holes appeared in the wall. Standing on tiptoes, I peeked through.

There was Annie's class, all gathered round their teacher. I suddenly realized I must be looking through the eyes of the painting. "You can spy on people," I whispered. "Someone's been watching us."

"It must be Cryptorum." Aiden peered through the eyeholes. "He never wanted the school to come here in the first place. He must be checking to see whether we're behaving and following his rules."

We crept further along. The passage branched off in three different directions. The right-hand corridor led straight to a set of stairs leading up. We took the middle passage and heard Mrs Perez's voice from the other side of the wall. Finding another round knob, I slid back the panel to look.

Mrs Perez was organizing the class into a circle. A woman I'd never seen before stood in the centre. She had flowing blonde hair and a fancy red-and-silver scarf around her neck. Her make-up made her look like a doll with very white skin and red lips.

"This is Miss Mason, everyone," said Mrs Perez. "She's our new music teacher and she's going to come here three or four times a week. Today she's come to teach you all the recorder."

I pulled a face and whispered to Aiden, "We're missing the recorder lesson." Miss Mason turned as I spoke and for a second I thought she'd looked right at me.

"Robyn, stop mucking around," Aiden hissed from further down the passage. "I've found the stairs to the basement."

The stairs were steep and we couldn't see the bottom. As we stared down into the darkness,

I suddenly wanted to change my mind about the whole thing. I was just about to tell Aiden when the floorboards creaked. Aiden nudged my arm and jerked his head. Something was coming up behind us.

It was too late to turn off the light. Either we could descend into darkness or wait here for whatever it was. As if to point out the problem, a long moan rose from the depths. The creature below sounded hungry.

Feet tapped on the wooden floor. Was this a spiny creature, a skeleton or a totally new and even deadlier kind of monster? A scratching sound added to the tapping, like a whole bunch of bony fingers scraping along the wall. How many monsters were there? We could be surrounded in seconds. The hairs on my arms rose as the floorboards creaked again – closer this time. I clenched my fists, eyes fixed on the bend in the passage.

Fingers curled around the corner … and I was pretty relieved when I saw they were human. A girl with two dark brown plaits and freckles appeared. She was the same girl that had been trying to look in the bat barn yesterday. She wasn't from our class but she looked tall enough to be from year five, the class below. Her eyes widened when she saw us.

"How did you get in here?" I said. "You nearly scared the life out of us."

"Sorry!" The girl gave an uncertain smile. "I found a door upstairs. It's behind a mirror – the one with birds all around the frame."

"See! I knew there'd be another door," I told Aiden and he rolled his eyes at me.

"I was following a weird-looking creature and then it just disappeared," the girl went on. "That's when I found the hidden door. I'm Nora Juniper."

"I'm Robyn and this is Aiden," I said. "What did the creature look like?"

"It was small but covered in lots of spines." Nora shook back her plaits. "I guess it looked a bit like a goblin—"

"Crossed with a porcupine," I finished. "So you can see freaky stuff too."

"And did you eat anything funny?" Aiden said eagerly. "Or did you leave something that everyone else was eating? Or did someone try to hypnotize you?"

Nora paled. "Er, I don't know! The vegetable soup my dad made for dinner last night tasted pretty strange but we all ate it, and I don't *think* I've been hypnotized."

"Yeah! I bet every hypnotized person says that."

Aiden started pacing up and down. "I don't get it. Why can we see these weird creatures? Why *us*?"

A smooth voice cut through the darkness. "It was destined for you to see these things from the moment you were born." Miss Smiting glided up behind Nora, her green eyes unblinking. "And that isss why we need you so very much."

"Need us for what?" My heart started thumping.

Miss Smiting didn't answer. Slipping past us, she descended into the dark. "Come!" she told us.

I exchanged looks with Aiden. Would it be completely crazy to follow Miss Smiting to the basement? Probably. But we had to find out what she knew. We went down the steep stairs to find a large wooden door at the bottom. Miss Smiting pressed some numbers on a keypad and the door swung open. Beyond that was another door. Miss Smiting took out a thick bunch of keys and turned them in three different locks. Beyond that was a gate made from metal bars which she carefully unbolted.

I've never liked being underground and I was already starting to sweat. "You really don't want us to get out again, do you?" I tried to joke.

Nora cast me a look of alarm.

"The doors and locksss are not for you," Miss Smiting said. "Well, not precisely."

That didn't exactly make me feel better.

Before I could ask what she meant, Miss Smiting flicked a switch and a row of fluorescent lights pinged on one after the other. We were in a massive stone cellar, littered with glass boxes and metal cages. The nearest cage contained nothing but a small pile of bones. I gulped. Had Miss Smiting let something die in there?

"Welcome to the dungeon," Miss Smiting said.

A chorus of growls and whines rose at the sound of her voice, ending in the long, low moan we'd heard before.

"What *is* that?" Nora's face turned even paler.

"That is a boggun." Miss Smiting pointed to a dark shape inside a glass case. "Try not to be afraid or disgusted. They feed on negative emotions."

I crept a bit closer and the creature unfolded into a tall, black figure. It had no face, just a flicker of eyes now and then. I shivered.

"JUNELLA!" Mr Cryptorum burst through the doors like thunder. His face was flushed and his hair was wilder than ever.

"Be calm, Erasmus," Miss Smiting said. "They'll hear you in the town square."

Cryptorum paced up and down. "What does it matter whether they hear me when you've brought half the school down here already?" He pointed to us. "Out! OUT!"

I decided no one had told Crytorum about the boggun feeding on negative emotions. "There's three of us," I told him. "So it's not half the school."

Aiden gave me a *shut up* sort of look and Nora hid behind him, which was easy for her as she was small.

Cryptorum glared from me to Miss Smiting. "After years of secrecy – carefully keeping everything to ourselves – why would you open this dungeon to anyone who wants to see? They'll lock us up as criminals. We'll be hounded out of town!"

Miss Smiting sighed. "They're not just anyone. There is a reason for everything, Erasmus, if you will just sssee some senssse!"

I was starting to get very nervous about why Miss Smiting wanted us down here. I glanced at Aiden. He and Nora had both edged closer to the door.

There was a clicking noise and something touched my sleeve. A bony arm had slid out of the nearest cage and stiff fingers closed around my wrist. I yelped and pulled at them with my free hand. The bony fingers tightened, crushing my skin.

Aiden dived in and together we prised each

finger open, but as soon as we got one loose the others clamped down even harder.

Suddenly, Cryptorum drew a silver blade out of nowhere and aimed a massive blow at the skeletal arm. It drew back through the bars of the cage and I glimpsed a scrawny white figure crouching there before the whole thing collapsed into a pile of bones again. Cryptorum tucked his blade into a sheath beneath his coat.

"What is that thing?" Aiden's hand shook. "It's the same creature that was in our classroom, isn't it?"

"WHAT?" Cryptorum roared. "You let a scree sag loose upstairs, Junella? Have you gone completely out of your mind?"

"I wass close by the whole time, watching them." Miss Smiting said.

I exchanged glances with Aiden. So it had been Miss Smiting watching through the eyes in the paintings.

"I had to know if they were Chimes," she continued. "I had their recordsss but I still had to be sure." She produced some sheets of paper. The top one had my name on it.

Miss Smiting handed Cryptorum the papers and he rifled through them, shaking his head. "Time of birth – it's hardly conclusive."

"That's why I checked." Her green eyes narrowed. "Tell them, Erasmus. You must tell them."

Another low moan rose from the glass case with the boggun inside.

"Tell us what?" I asked.

Cryptorum looked at me, Aiden and Nora from under lowered eyebrows. His face softened a little. "You were born as the clock chimed midnight. That's why you can see the creatures of the Unseen World. You are Chimes – like I am."

Mr Cryptorum
Follows the Bats

he words went round and round in my
head: *You were born as the clock chimed
midnight.* Mum had once told me I was
born in the middle of the night but I'd
never thought much about it before.

"Wait – what did you call us?" I said.

Cryptorum's eyebrows lowered. "Chimes."

"Can I look at those?" Aiden took the papers
from Mr Cryptorum. He passed me the one with
my name on it and I stared at the squiggly writing:
TIME OF BIRTH: 12:00 A.M.

"So we were born at midnight," I said. "What
difference does that make?"

"No one knows why being born at that exact
time gives you special sight, but your powers were

dormant until you heard the midnight chiming of a Mortal Clock." Cryptorum frowned at Miss Smiting. "I shouldn't have let you persuade me to have it mended. I expected an adult – maybe a teenager – not a bunch of kids."

"I've been through most of the records of birthsss and found no other adult born at midnight," Miss Smiting replied. "And children will be more – how do you say? – open of mind."

I stared at Cryptorum in disbelief. What did he mean by a Mortal Clock? I was about to ask when the clock on the tower began striking two. It was a deep, powerful sound.

"You mean that clock outside has something to do with this?" Aiden asked.

"You have special sight because you were born at midnight, but you must also be called to your abilities on the strike of twelve," Cryptorum told us. "Only a Mortal Clock has the power to do that, and there aren't very many of them in the world. The clockmakers of Prague discovered how to make them and passed the craft on in secret, one Chime to another, for hundreds of years."

I rubbed my aching forehead. This was so strange – almost too much to take in. But I knew I'd woken up and heard the Grimdean clock strike midnight a few days ago. I remembered going to the window and seeing the spiny thing for the first time that night too.

"Then these creatures are definitely real," Nora said in a small voice.

"Of course they're real!" Cryptorum strode down the cellar, pointing to each cage. "Scree sag, boggun, kobolds." One of the kobolds growled and I recognized them as the spiny things I'd seen outside my house. "Some monsters, like the kobold, are little more than an annoyance, but others are deadly."

"Which ones?" I asked.

"There's no need for you to know. There's no need for you to have seen *any* of this." He scowled at Miss Smiting who gave a faint hiss.

"What about all the other people in the world who were born at midnight?" Nora asked. "We can't be the only ones."

"That is true. But many people never hear the sound of a Mortal Clock and those that do often put their new sight down to an overactive imagination. They tell themselves that their mind is playing tricks on them, that a spiky kobold is just a prickly bush or an oddly shaped dog. A boggun seems like just another shadow." Cryptorum folded his arms. "You will stop seeing monsters after a while too.

Go back to your normal lives and forget all about today."

"I can't!" I burst out. "We had a kobold in our kitchen. It could've hurt my family!"

"For goodness' sake, girl! Kobolds can do little more than bite and scratch. They are the least of my worries."

I scowled. The kobold had seemed pretty scary at the time, especially as none of my family could see it.

Cryptorum shook his head. "Go back upstairs, all three of you, and do *not* breathe a word of this place or what's in here to anyone!"

"No one would believe us anyway," Aiden said. "And how can we forget about all this when we don't know what monster we might see next?"

"I know I won't forget." Nora bit her lip.

"You must!" Cryptorum turned to Miss Smiting, saying fiercely, "Take them out of here, Junella. I will not be part of this ridiculous scheme."

Miss Smiting hissed and a thin green tongue darted out of her mouth. "See reason, Erasmusss! You are too old to be doing all thisss on your own – tracking monsters and fighting. Remember when you hurt your leg last month chasing after a scree sag? You are not as young as you used to be!"

For a minute I thought that Mr Cryptorum was going to storm out, but then he sank on to a wooden crate. His shoulders slumped. "It's the responsibility!" he muttered. "It's been my sacred duty to protect the town. I cannot ask anyone else to do what I've done all these years."

"Then show them what to do and let them choose for themselves." Miss Smiting put a hand on his shoulder. "It's time!"

He nodded slowly. "You're right. I'm getting too old. But these are just children."

I stiffened. I was still annoyed that he'd snapped at me about the kobold in my kitchen. How was I supposed to know it wasn't that dangerous? How many other kids had been scared by some creature while everyone told them there was nothing there? It didn't seem fair. My head ached. It didn't help that the kobold really stank.

"They need air." Miss Smiting eyed me closely. "Take them to your study, Erasmus. I will tell your teachersss. . . What shall I say? I need a good excuse. Something that they will like."

"Tell them you're setting us a special project to be done after school," Nora said. "Teachers always like the sound of that."

*

We heard Miss Smiting speaking to Mrs Lovell as we followed Cryptorum through the hidden door behind the mirror on the first floor. "You see, Mr Cryptorum has been wishing to monitor the wildlife in the grounds for years," she was saying. "We have selected three pupilsss to assist us. . ."

Cryptorum led us through the upstairs rooms and corridors. There were long galleries hung with paintings leading to parlours with grand pianos and flowery sofas. Everywhere we went, there were mirrors on the walls. We climbed another flight of stairs and came to a landing where the corridor branched off in two directions. On the right, tropical plants in reddish-brown pots stretched their fan-shaped leaves to the ceiling. The left-hand corridor looked very bare.

"Those are Miss Smiting's rooms." Cryptorum nodded to the passage with the plants. "And these are mine." He opened the first door.

The room was a large study, with shelves full of books and a musty smell of paper. Above the fireplace was a painting of a man and a woman in posh clothes. The man looked so much like Cryptorum that I guessed they might be his parents. Next to the painting was a small white cupboard with a key in the lock.

A desk stood by the window. Out in the garden Josh's class were doing PE while a man with grey hair pushed a wheelbarrow round the edge of the lawn. I leant closer to the window to get a better view, and jumped as a little crab-like creature scuttled across the desk, weaving past a photo of Cryptorum, Miss Smiting and a woman with curly hair. The whole of the creature's shell was covered by an unblinking blue eye.

"Don't worry. That's just Eye," Cryptorum told me. "He won't hurt you. He was a vampire's pet until I rescued him."

The thought of the creature as a pet made my head whirl. I watched it run down the leg of the desk and disappear underneath.

"Sit down." Cryptorum waved to a brown leather sofa. He locked the white cupboard and pocketed the key before seating himself in the armchair opposite. I didn't think I'd ever seen his eyebrows look so wild and bristly. It was like they had a life of their own.

Aiden, Nora and me looked at each other. Then we sat together on the sofa.

Cryptorum stared into the empty fireplace. I nudged Aiden. I couldn't stand this silence.

"Stop it, Robyn!" Aiden whispered.

75

"What's that?" Cryptorum fixed us with a glare. "How can you expect to become a Chime if you can't sit still for five minutes? It requires skill, hours of practice and great bravery."

I gripped the edge of the sofa, longing to tell him that if he didn't think we were good enough he should just let us go, but two things stopped me. First, he was looking pretty fierce. Second, I wanted to know more about what a Chime did.

"How do you know we're not brave?" The words popped out before I could stop them. I felt Aiden twitch beside me.

Cryptorum's eyebrows rose. "What's your name?"

"Robyn," I said. "And this is Aiden and Nora."

Rising to his feet, Cryptorum began to pace up and down.

I whispered to Aiden. "This was your idea. I'm missing a recorder lesson for this!"

Aiden rolled his eyes. "You were the one that wouldn't wait till tomorrow."

"Guys," Nora muttered. "Look at the bats!"

A black shape swooped past the window, then another. Cryptorum leant close to the glass, muttering something under his breath. He turned, his hand on the sheathed blade that hung under his coat. "You mustn't go anywhere until I return. Do you understand?"

"What about lessons?" Aiden started to say, but Cryptorum was already out the door.

I went to the window. A cloud of bats was flocking at the far end of the garden. More bats poured from beneath the roof of the barn, joining the whirling mass, and then they zoomed away towards the edge of town.

"I don't get it!" I peered out. "What are the bats up to? Why does Cryptorum keep them?"

Aiden joined me at the window. "It's definitely weird that he left so fast."

"*That's* weird?!" I said. "What about the monsters in the basement? What about the eye-thing he keeps as a pet? The woman with the green tongue and lizard eyes who runs his house? There's a billion things about this that are weird. You could make that man Emperor of Weirdness! You don't even need to mention him leaving fast."

Aiden grinned. "Just breathe, OK? At least we're starting to get some answers."

"You mean that we're special because we were born at midnight? That's the craziest answer ever!"

"It looks like the bats help him," Nora said suddenly.

"Wait – what?" I stared.

Nora was standing by the bookcase looking through a large, leather-bound book. "You said why does he keep the bats. They help him." She turned another page. "Bats have echolocation, which means they bounce sounds off things to find their way around. Looks like they use a similar method to find creatures of the Unseen World. The monsters give off a vibration that we can't detect – but the bats can sense it. That's what it says in this guide to Chiropterology."

My mouth dropped open.

Nora shelved the book and picked up another one. She opened it at the first page. "Hey, this one has a bunch of useful information... *Where Chimes come from.*" She started reading aloud. "*The first Mortal Clock was invented by accident by the master clockmaker Josef Dusek of Prague when the grandfather clock he was making was struck by lightning in 1405. Josef happened to be a Chime himself, and as soon as the clock struck midnight he was able to perceive the creatures of the Unseen World. For the next three hundred years, Chimes often took up the same craft, and a hidden fellowship of Chimes passing as clockmakers developed.*"

"So they all sat around making these Mortal

Clocks," I said. "Not exactly brave and adventurous, is it?"

Nora flicked a look at me and carried on reading. "*Their first major challenge was stopping the spread of vampires across Europe during the years of the Black Death, a terrible disease that ravaged the fourteenth century.*"

"Good to know they did something useful." I joined her by the shelf and ran my finger across the books. Most were very old – many had broken spines and brown pages. I didn't understand half the titles but a few looked interesting – ones on enchantment, beasts and the undead.

I picked a book called *Enchantments and Illusions in the Unseen World* and opened a random page. "*Edible spells can be hidden in many foods,*" I read out. "That's crazy! There are spells you can actually eat."

"Ooh, can I see that?" Nora asked so I handed her the book. "Amazing! You can prevent an edible spell from working by biting into the food but not swallowing it..."

I'd stopped listening properly because I'd seen a book on the top shelf with a beautiful silver sword on the spine. I got on tiptoes to pull it down. It was titled: *Super Sword Moves that can Save your Life.* "Hey, Aiden," I said. "This is awesome!"

"No, *this* is awesome!" Aiden held up a large bow. "Look how perfectly this has been made. I bet you can shoot a really long way with it." He slotted an arrow against the wood.

"Where did you get that?" I put down the book.

"Here by the desk." Aiden pointed.

"You shouldn't touch that." Nora looked nervous. "What if Mr Cryptorum comes back?"

"I bet he won't be back for ages." I glanced out of the window. The bats weren't flocking over the trees any more, but there was no sign of Cryptorum. I took the bow from Aiden.

"Hey! Watch the trigger," Aiden said.

My finger knocked the arrow before he'd said it. The bow string twanged and the arrow whooshed through the air. It landed right in the forehead of the man in the painting – the man that was probably Cryptorum's father.

There was a horrible silence.

Cryptorum came striding out of the trees at the bottom of the garden. He glared at the children doing PE.

Aiden and me dived for the arrow at the same time. We pulled and pulled but it wouldn't move. Pushing a chair up to the fireplace, I climbed on and tried to wrench the arrow free.

Nora ran to the window. "He's coming back! Hurry!"

I tugged harder. "I . . . can't . . . get . . . it . . . out!" I muttered between clenched teeth.

A door slammed downstairs.

Me, Nora and Aiden looked at each other. "He can't kill us as easily if we're back in our classrooms," I gasped. "Run!"

Our New Club
Has the Dumbest
Name Ever

hen we got back to class we found the music teacher had already gone. I couldn't stop glancing at the door and I couldn't concentrate on the capital cities of the world, which Mrs Perez was trying to teach us. I had that horrible squirming feeling that you get in your stomach when you've done something wrong. What would Cryptorum do when he got back to his study and found an arrow sticking out of the picture of his dad?

A few minutes before the end of school I whispered to Aiden, "I have to go and tell him it was me. If I don't come back alive then you can have my light-up pen with the ink eraser and my glow-in-the-dark felt tips."

"Don't be daft. He won't kill you," Aiden said.

I wasn't so sure.

"So, Robyn," said Mrs Perez, who'd spotted me whispering, "tell me what you're going to be doing after school with Miss Smiting and Mr Cryptorum. How did you get picked for that anyway?"

"Um . . . we were really helpful to Mr Cryptorum and this is our reward," I said, making it up on the spot.

Mrs Perez nodded. "I hear it's a nature study, so what will you be looking for. . . ?"

I stared at her. A kobold, a scree sag and a boggun. Well, I couldn't say that.

"Mostly bats, miss," Aiden said quickly. "Mr Cryptorum loves them. That's why he keeps them in that barn in the garden."

"You have been so helpful, children." Miss Smiting had entered noiselessly and was standing in the doorway behind us. "And that isss why we would like to turn it into a regular club. So we will sssee you after school starting from tomorrow."

Mrs Perez looked surprised, as if she'd expected us to have messed up. "Well done, Robyn and Aiden. I'm glad that this after-school activity will be a regular thing for you. Don't forget to tell your parents that you'll be staying late." She closed her textbook with a snap. "Home time! Pack up your things, everyone."

There was a rush of scraping chairs and things being stuffed in bags. Hector checked that Mrs Perez wasn't listening before leaning over. "You're going to Bat Club! That is so lame."

Sally-Anne was smirking too and my cheeks reddened. "Wow, Hector," I snapped back. "Is that the best you can do for an insult?" I shoved past him and caught up with Miss Smiting in the hallway. "Um, about the arrow..."

She studied me. There was a hint of a smile in her green eyes. "I have removed it. In future you will not touch a bow indoors. Iss that clear?"

I nodded. "I'm really sorry."

"Being sorry afterwards iss no good to me, Robyn Silver." She added in a lower voice. "No need to mention thisss to Mr Cryptorum." Then she glided away down the corridor.

I grinned. I had to admit I thought she was pretty cool.

As Aiden and me made our way to the front entrance, the news about "Bat Club" was already beginning to spread to kids in other classes. I reckoned we mostly had Sally-Anne to thank for all the people muttering and shooting looks at us. She loved spreading gossip. Luckily, some kid got out a yoghurt which exploded on the front steps, and everyone forgot about us after that.

As we walked down Demus Street, the clock on the Grimdean tower began its deep, powerful chiming. It's golden face and hands glowed in the afternoon sunlight. I decided I would go to the club. Now I knew what kind of horrid things were out there, I figured it only made sense that I learnt how to defend myself. I was still freaked out though. I wasn't sure which was weirder – knowing that monsters really existed or knowing I was one of the special ones who could see them. I'd never been special before. Not at anything. If Aiden hadn't been there too I would've thought I'd dreamt it.

Mum made a roast dinner that night. Dad wasn't home yet but we started without him. Rain was whipping against the window and the kitchen boiler was making its usual rumbling sound as the tiny orange light flickered into life.

I watched Josh take five stuffing balls from the dish and hide them in his lap under the table. There were supposed to be two each, but I had bigger things to worry about. I was looking for my moment to mention Bat Club. I waited till Mum came to the table with a dish of carrots. "I'm staying for a club tomorrow, so I'll be back late," I said.

"What's that, honey?" Mum put down the dish. "Ben, don't take all the roast potatoes. The rest of us want some."

"It's just they're so nice," Ben said, spooning them straight from the serving dish into his mouth.

"Annie, why don't you let me pour that? What were you saying, Robyn?" Mum turned back to me.

I opened my mouth to try again.

"I got another merit at school today," Sammie butted in, "for my history assignment."

"That's brilliant!" Mum beamed.

"So . . . can I dye my hair?" Sammie carried on. "Petra's done hers purple and it looks really nice."

"I'm staying late at a club tomorrow," I said again.

"Don't INTERRUPT!" Sammie snapped at me. "I was talking first."

I glared. "No you weren't!"

"Girls, don't start arguing," Mum sighed. "What sort of club, Robyn?"

"It's a sort of nature thing," I said. "Mr Cryptorum's running it."

"It's called Bat Club!" Annie piped up.

My heart sank down to the floor. Annie must have heard all the gossip on the way out of school. There was no way Sammie would let this go. "It isn't just about the bats. It's about lots of other creatures too," I said. At least that part was true. "Aiden's joined as well. So can I go?"

Mum added some carrots to Annie's plate before sitting down. "And this club is really called Bat Club? It's an actual club – not just something you and Aiden have cooked up between you?"

I gritted my teeth. "It's a real club." I couldn't bring myself to say Bat Club.

"Can I go?" asked Annie.

"Bat Club!" Sammie grinned. "Bats for the batty! Suits you perfectly, Robyn."

Ben laughed. This annoyed me. He hardly ever took Sammie's side over mine.

Mum shot me a look as she helped herself to some peas. "I don't know. By the time you leave Grimdean House it'll be dark, and I don't want you walking around on your own that late."

"I'll walk back with Aiden so I won't be on my own," I said.

"Why do you want to go anyway?" Mum frowned. "I wouldn't have expected you to want to spend more time at school. If you're staying late so you can muck around you should leave the space at the club for the younger ones."

"Like me!" Annie spooned her carrots back into the serving dish.

"Annie, don't do that!" Mum said. The back door opened and Dad tramped in, his blue boiler suit covered in rain spots. "There you are! I was starting to think they'd never let you come home."

I reached for the dish of peas. Maybe if Mum saw me eating vegetables she'd be nicer about letting me come home late. Unluckily I knocked the dish with my arm and tipped it over, sending peas rolling off the table on to the floor.

"Robyn! Get a brush and sweep those up. Honestly! Every dinner time food ends up everywhere." Mum sighed.

I made a face and grabbed the brush.

"Ugh – rotten day!" Dad rubbed a towel over his damp hair. "We had to help sort out damaged power line poles on the edge of town near Blagdurn Heath. Something's damaged them – taken chunks out of the wood all the way to the top."

Mum got a plate for him and started filling it with food. "Was it vandals?"

"No, not unless they can climb the poles." Dad took the seat at the end of the table. "This old guy who lives nearby told us that giant porcupines have been spotted on the heath." He gave a short laugh. "So it must be wood-eating porcupines causing all the damage. Either that or squirrels with steel-plated teeth!"

I was only half listening. I *had* to get my parents to let me stay for the club but there was no way I could tell them what it was really about. I stared at the potatoes on my plate. I'd been born at midnight and this was my chance to find out if I'd be any good as a Chime. Sammie was always coming home with ace report cards and doing competitions at her gym club. Ben was one of the best runners in the county and even Josh played football. Annie was the cute one and got loads of attention for being the youngest, but I'd never done anything good. I was just Robyn the disaster zone – the one who knocked stuff over and made a mess.

Now I had this one special thing – the first time I'd ever been important – and I couldn't even tell them.

Sammie was arguing with Mum about dying her hair. I could see Mum starting to weaken. Sammie does this – just goes on and on and on until people give in. The problem was that once Mum gave in on one thing it got tricky to persuade her about anything else. I had to get in there first. If I could get Dad on my side, that might work.

"So can I go to the nature club after school?" I interrupted loudly. "Mrs Perez thought it would be a really good idea. Me and Aiden got chosen over everyone else in our class and we'll be learning stuff about frogs and owls and mice and insects." I had no idea whether you could find all those animals in the Grimdean garden but I carried on anyway. I needed one more push – something to make the club sound really educational. What was that thing Nora had said about the bats?

"I think I'll learn loads." I gave my parents an innocent, wide-eyed look. "The bats that live in the barn there use echolocation to fly around."

They all stared at me. Even Sammie looked surprised for a second.

"What's this about a club?" Dad asked.

I repeated what I'd said to Mum, throwing in some extra words like habitat and hibernation.

"I don't see why she shouldn't go," Dad said. "Aren't we always telling them to try and learn something at school?"

"All right, you can go," Mum told me taking a crumbled stuffing ball out of Josh's lap. "Sammie, I don't want you dying your hair some horrible colour. I know your school won't like it and they'll probably send a letter home. No, that's final."

Sammie shot me a poisonous look as if it was my fault. She caught up with me on the stairs after dinner. "You're such a little freak – joining a Bat Club! I know you're just doing it for attention."

I laughed. "Yeah, whatever."

"Showing off with your echolocation. I bet you don't even know what it means."

She was right. I thought it had something to do with echoes but I wasn't exactly sure. I reached the top of the stairs and went into my bedroom, but Sammie still wouldn't leave me alone.

"You're such a baby! No wonder you have to share a room with Annie." She stomped off.

"I'm just glad I don't share one with you," I said, mostly to myself. "I wish I didn't have to share a house with you either." The wish bubble popped out of my mouth and drifted slowly through the air. I watched it in surprise. So much had happened today that I'd almost forgotten that seeing wishes was one of my new talents.

This wish wasn't like the ones I'd made with Annie, though. It had a dark, glassy surface – so dark that it was hard to see the picture of the wish inside. I caught a glimpse of Sammie leaving our house dragging a suitcase behind her, and my stomach lurched. It was only a wish though. It was Sammie's fault for making me cross enough to say it.

I Fight with a Frostblade for the Very First Time

By lunchtime the next day, half the kids at school had asked Mrs Lovell if they could join Bat Club. Even Hector had tried to persuade her to let him go. Kids were talking about it in the corridors and wish bubbles were floating around with little pictures of bats inside.

As we ate lunch Sally-Anne told us she'd seen the headmistress go up to Mr Cryptorum in the entrance hall to ask whether he could let more children into his nature club.

"He said he already had plenty of people," Sally-Anne said. "He was kind of snappish actually. How can three people be enough for a club?"

"I think it's because the bats don't like a lot of

noise," Aiden said. "If there were more people it would just disturb them."

I was pretty impressed with this quick thinking. It worried me a bit though. If Cryptorum really was using the bats to help him would he expect us to go into the barn and get close to them? I didn't really like the bats with their little beady eyes and flappy wings.

As we left the dining room, we saw Miss Mason, the music teacher arriving with a sparkling smile. Her red lipstick was bright against her pale skin and she wore a purple sequinned jacket and high-heeled boots. "Are you ready for a musical afternoon?" she asked us. "I've got shakers, triangles and a xylophone for you to play!"

There was a roar further down the corridor. "There are too many children," growled Cryptorum. "And Too Much Noise!"

Miss Mason's smile faltered. "I'll just fetch the sheet music!" She dashed back down the steps. It was funny to see a teacher as nervous of Mr Cryptorum's temper as we were!

News about Bat Club continued to be the hot gossip inside Grimdean House all afternoon, When home time came, a gaggle of kids hung around near the garden hoping to tag along. Miss

Smiting firmly shooed them out of the building, her long skirt brushing the floor. "Off you go now or Mr Cryptorum will turn you all into bat snacks!"

"So much for training secretly so that no one gets suspicious!" growled Cryptorum once the kids had streamed out of the front door.

"Hush, Erasmusss!" Miss Smiting told him. "They are just curious children. We can do many thingsss to throw them off the smell."

"Off the scent?" said Nora.

She smiled. "That'ss right."

I caught a glimpse of Miss Smiting's thin green tongue behind her teeth. A mass of questions boiled inside my brain. "Miss Smiting, are you actually human?" I blurted out just as the clock on the tower began to chime. "And do the bats really help to find monsters? Is that why they flew off somewhere yesterday?"

Cryptorum glared at me and for a second I thought he was going to send me away like the other kids. "Enough of these silly questions! We don't have time for chit-chat."

Aiden's forehead creased. "But, sir! I just want to ask one thing. Isn't it strange that Robyn and me are friends and we're both Chimes?"

"That's not strange at all," Cryptorum said. "On some unconscious level you sensed you were alike in a very important way – that's why you became friends. Now follow me!"

Cryptorum took us out into the garden and across the leaf-covered lawn. I followed a bit sulkily. How come Aiden got his question answered while mine were just silly? I didn't like it when grown-ups played favourites.

The sun was sinking below the nearby houses in a blaze of orange. One lonely bat flew over the garden, wheeled into the sky and returned with a slow flap of its wings.

I decided to try again. "So do the bats really help you with their echo . . . their echo-thingy?"

"Echo-location," Nora said.

"We'll get to all that in good time," Cryptorum rumbled.

There was a tiny movement at the edge of the barn. Cryptorum was over there in a second. He pulled Hector out of the shadows and marched him back to the house with one hand on his shoulder.

"I was just looking for my football," Hector protested. "I lost it at lunchtime. I'll tell my dad!"

"Tell him. He knows where I live," Cryptorum said grimly. "This garden is out of bounds after school time to you and everyone else unless I say otherwise."

"I'll see him out." The grey-haired gardener hobbled out of the little side garden which was surrounded by tall hedges.

"Thank you, Obediah." Cryptorum nodded. "Then leave all your other jobs till tomorrow. You've done plenty for today."

Obediah Brown nodded and escorted a red-faced Hector up the marble steps. The single bat flapped past and I ducked, feeling the draught from its wings. The creature circled round and swooped under the roof of the barn.

Cryptorum watched the bat disappear. "No more humans are here, so we're safe to proceed." He led us to the bottom of the garden where a stone bench stood beside a shed. Cryptorum pointed to the bench and we sat down. The wind swept down the long garden, peeling handfuls of leaves from the trees.

Cryptorum studied us closely. "This is your last chance to change your mind. The midnight bell of the Mortal Clock woke up your second sight, but you do not have to lead the life of a Chime." He looked from Nora to Aiden and me. "Many people like us close their eyes to the monsters and convince themselves they're imagining the things in the shadows. They trick their minds until they cannot see the creatures any more. Not many people embrace their gift – it's little wonder, really." He turned and unlocked the shed. The door swung open to reveal a row of gleaming silver swords, each one long and stick-thin. Above them was a rack of wooden bows alongside a container full of arrows.

"You may want to forget too," he continued. "You could go back home and never speak of this again. Soon you will stop seeing the kobolds and the scree sags. You will stop hearing the boggun's moan. You won't even notice how extraordinary Junella is any more." He nodded to Miss Smiting. "This life isn't easy. I got the gift at thirteen after my parents hired a craftsman to fit a clock to our tower. By fifteen I'd run away from Wendleton, driven to desperation by trying to keep the town safe from monsters. My father and mother did not understand, and how could I explain it to them?"

"Where did you go?" I asked.

"I travelled south – I wanted to get as far away from my troubles as I could – but all I met were more monsters. At last I reached the Amazon river where I met an amazing person – half woman and half snake. She showed me how to survive in the rainforest. That was more than fifty years ago."

Miss Smiting gave a faint hiss, her green eyes alight. "It does not ssseem such a very long time."

So Miss Smiting was half snake. I guess it explained a lot.

"At last I learned to live with danger – I found my courage," Cryptorum continued. "But you still have a choice. You can still live an ordinary life – forget what you saw in my basement and go home." He looked at us searchingly. "But whatever you choose, you *must* keep the Chime world secret. Telling people of monsters they cannot see would only cause panic, and that could be dangerous for them and for you."

My stomach was doing somersaults. I was scared but not scared enough to go home. "I don't want to forget what I've seen," I said. "I want to know how to fight."

"I want to know how to use those." Aiden was staring at the wooden bows in the shed.

Nora hesitated, before adding, "I'm staying too."

Cryptorum nodded. "All right. Then the first thing you need to know is how to handle a blade." He took three swords out of the shed, handing one to each of us. "These are frostblades and they're made from silver. The name comes from the pale colour of the metal."

I took the sword. It had a wooden handle bound with leather and the blade was amazingly thin and light, almost like those weapons they use in fencing. If my family had been here they would have freaked at the sight of me – disaster-area Robyn – holding a sharp blade.

The funny thing was I didn't feel like I was going to drop it or do anything stupid. Holding it felt like the most normal thing in the world. I twisted my hand gently to flick the blade in a sideways figure of eight. The sword made a swooshing noise as it moved.

Aiden was trying out his weapon too. "It doesn't look much like the swords you see on TV."

Cryptorum closed the shed door and drew his sword from the sheath beneath his jacket. "It's not made for fighting humans. Silver isn't a strong metal but it has certain qualities that make monsters fear it."

"Is it because it's so shiny?" I guessed. "And expensive?"

"Silver has the highest electrical conductivity and thermal conductivity of any metal," Nora told us.

We all looked at her.

"If the creatures of the Unseen World have a high electrical voltage then it's possible that being pierced with a silver blade weakens their life force and makes them easier to defeat," she added.

I lowered my blade. How did Nora know all this stuff? It was hard to believe she was in the year below us.

"Well I'm not a scientist but I know that monsters can be beaten by a frostblade," Cryptorum told us. "It pierces them like nothing else I've ever tried. I made these many years ago."

Miss Smiting put a hand on his arm. "I shall go. I mussst move the kobolds out of the dungeon." She glided back towards the house.

"Why is she moving the kobolds?" I asked.

"Because they're not dangerous enough to kill someone. They just need to be taken somewhere wild – far away from humans – and released." Cryptorum snapped. "Now stop asking questions and *listen*!"

"Sorry!" I longed to ask whether they let the bogguns and the scree sags out too. I hoped the answer was no.

"So here are the most essential sword moves. Watch closely." Cryptorum demonstrated each movement in slow motion. Then he made us repeat them at the same speed until he was sure we'd got it.

We twisted, blocked, sliced and jabbed. Cryptorum had a name for every move – stuff like the short-hand parry which basically involved blocking someone else's attack. I knew I wouldn't remember the names but everything else was easy. It felt like the frostblade was part of my body, and its movement flowed like water into my fingers, along my arms and all the way down to my feet. The dying sunlight glinted on my sword as I moved. It was a bit like dancing.

When the garden grew dark, Cryptorum switched on the shed light. Then he took out three leather jackets and told us to put them on.

"Sir, this doesn't fit," I said, trying to find my hands at the ends of the way-too-big sleeves.

"Just make the best of it, Robyn," Cryptorum growled. "You need some basic protection if you're going to fight each other. You and Nora pair up. Aiden, you can practise against me. Take turns to attack and defend."

I faced Nora and flexed my arms, trying to get used to the stupid leather jacket. Nora was shorter than me so her jacket looked even sillier. I took up a blocking position. "OK, you go first."

She hesitated. When she moved, I saw straight away where her thrust was aiming. I parried, hitting the sword out of her hand. I was pleased but I didn't want to show it – Nora was smaller after all. "OK I was lucky that time. Want to try again?"

Nora scrambled for her sword. One of her plaits had come loose and she suddenly looked even younger than usual. She tried again – a side swipe this time. I blocked her blow and knocked her blade to the ground a second time. She flushed and picked it up again. She wasn't any better at defending either. It was like fighting a kitten.

I looked up to find Cryptorum watching. "Swap over," he told us. "Aiden you fight Nora. Robyn, you're with me."

We swapped. I faced Mr Cryptorum with my sword ready, and the wind whistled down the garden, ruffling his mane of grey hair. I tried a sharp jab to the side but he swung round, blocking it easily. So I went for a high slicing movement. He brought his sword down on my shoulder and I winced. The tough leather of the jacket took most of the blow.

So it went on. Thrust – block – slice – parry.

The rhythm beat through me as I ducked and turned and swung the blade.

At last, Cryptorum stepped back. "Enough! You've done well – all of you."

I let my frostblade drop to my side and tried to get my breath back. My heart was racing, like, two hundred beats a minute, but I felt proud. I'd actually been good at this. Amazingly. No one would ever have expected it, especially not me.

As I helped Cryptorum put the frostblades away, I spotted a beautiful sword hanging at the far end of the shed. It was thicker than the ones we'd been using and it had swirly markings down the blade. "That one looks amazing." I pointed to it. "Can I try it out?"

"No, you can't!" Cryptorum scowled. "That's my best blade. I was given it by a man whose ancestor fought monsters during the time of Shakespeare."

I didn't argue but I ran my hand across the hilt of the sword when he wasn't looking. It was the coolest thing I'd ever seen.

"You were really good," Aiden said as we walked home afterwards. "I watched you at the end against Cryptorum and you were matching all his moves."

"I think he was holding back a bit." I rubbed my shoulder which was starting to ache.

"Yeah, he probably was. But still, for a first go you were awesome."

"Thanks." I grinned, my stomach flipping over. I'd been good at something. Me!

"I told Cryptorum that I wanted to stay when I saw those bows," Aiden went on. "But I'm not sure about this at all. The fact is, if the world is full of monsters, just training a few people isn't going to make much of a difference. Cryptorum needs a whole army."

A hedge rustled and we both swung round really fast. My hand clenched as if it missed the frostblade. Leaves parted and a whiskery nose poked out. We both relaxed – it was just a cat.

"At least learning to fight them is a start," I said.

"I guess." Aiden frowned. "But I don't know how much help Nora will be. She kept dropping her sword and her swing was pretty slow."

I felt a bit sorry for Nora. "Maybe she'll be better with a bow and arrow. See you tomorrow." I turned down my street, ran down the side passage and let myself in the back door. The kitchen was steamy and smelt of pizza. My favourite. Annie was eating a jacket potato – she never had any pizza because she didn't like cheese.

I grinned. "Is it pizza for tea?"

"Robyn! I forgot you were staying for your club. Did you have a nice time?" Mum asked.

"Yeah it was good." I scanned the empty plates and my stomach gurgled. "You did save me some, didn't you?"

Mum got up and checked inside the oven in a flustered way. "Sorry, honey. I completely forgot you were coming back later. I've got half a slice I didn't finish so you can have that."

I stared at the half-eaten slice. I couldn't believe they hadn't noticed I wasn't there. Pizza was my favourite meal and they'd eaten the WHOLE THING without me.

Sammie smirked. "It was delicious! Best pizza I've had for ages."

"Why don't I whip you up some scrambled eggs," Mum said. "Careful! Ben's running kit is right—"

It was too late. I tripped over the sports bag and sprawled across the floor. Sammie giggled as I picked myself up. If only they'd seen me earlier doing all those great sword moves. I sighed. It would be so awesome to tell them and see the sneer wiped off Sammie's face, but my new identity as a Chime had to remain secret – it was safer that way.

To my family I had to carry on being disaster-area Robyn.

Aiden Invents Some
Awesome Gadgets

Aiden, Nora and me stayed after school for Bat Club every day that week. On the third day, Mr Cryptorum set large round targets out on the lawn and taught us how to use the bows and arrows. We were using practice arrows, but the real ones were tipped with silver, Cryptorum told us, the same as the swords.

I found using a bow a bit harder than the sword. I tried to keep up with Aiden, who was firing off arrows really fast and hitting the target every time. Nora's first two arrows met her target. Then she sent one sideways and it hit the wall of the barn with a massive *thud*. A swarm of bats poured out of the roof and flew away into the distance.

"Oops!" Nora pulled a sorry face. "I didn't mean to do that."

Mr Cryptorum's eyebrows bristled and he moved us all down to the far end of the garden, well away from the barn.

I positioned my next arrow against the string, lined it up with the target and released. The arrow whizzed through the air, hitting the target just below the bullseye. "Hey! Did you see that! That was my best shot so far."

"Hmm?" Aiden wasn't looking at me. He was examining the bow. "I'd like to work on this. I bet I could make it shoot further."

"He'll never let you." I glanced over to where Cryptorum was trying to help Nora aim better.

"Maybe." Aiden got that determined look that meant he was planning to do something anyway.

By the beginning of our third week at Grimdean House, I was starting to feel like I knew my way around the place. The other kids in class had stopped asking us about Bat Club, although I sometimes caught Sally-Anne watching us curiously as we slipped out to the garden at the end of school.

Everyone else seemed to have grown used to the place too. Josh and his little friends became so brave they decided to sneak into one of the rooms marked KEEP OUT. Luckily, Miss Smiting had a knack of knowing exactly when they were going to try. After their fifth attempt, she took them to the bat barn and promised them they'd be cleaning it out if she caught them again. The place was thick with droppings so they gave up after that.

As she was banned from all the rooms marked KEEP OUT too, Mrs Lovell set up her Headmistress's office in front of the large wooden chest in the entrance hall. She put out two plastic chairs, a filing cabinet and a desk with a tiny cactus on it. Then she surrounded the whole thing with a blotchy green curtain hung on a metal rail like the kind you get in a hospital. Each time the clock on the tower made a deafening chime, the curtain would shake and she'd jump up in shock saying, "Oh my goodness!"

On Wednesday after school I crept downstairs by myself, leaving Aiden and Nora up in the north wing. Nora had her head buried in one of Cryptorum's dusty old books, and Aiden was working on something in one of the empty rooms. He'd been rushing off at breaks and lunchtimes all week. I'd seen him like this before when he was in the middle of making something. Aiden's dad was an engineer and, though they didn't see each other much because his parents were separated, he'd taught Aiden all kinds of practical stuff. I knew better than to try and interrupt till he'd got to the end.

Grimdean felt even creepier now it was almost empty. I pushed aside the tapestry in the ballroom and opened the hidden door. I wanted to see the creatures in the dungeon again. The passage inside the walls was deathly quiet, but when I reached the basement the key I'd borrowed from Cryptorum's study wouldn't unlock the door.

A boggun's groan echoed inside, making the door rattle. Were there more keys somewhere? In Cryptorum's desk maybe? If we were going to fight these monsters we had to face them some time.

"Robyn, dear." Miss Smiting had glided noiselessly up to me, making me jump. "Come back to the north wing. Mr Cryptorum has some new thingss to tell you."

I stifled a sigh. Every time we stayed indoors for Bat Club, Mr Cryptorum would drone on for hours about Chime stuff. Last week he'd gone on and on about how the bats were especially useful for tracking down feeding vampires, except there weren't any vampires left in Wendleton so the whole thing seemed pointless. The day before that he'd told us how the mirrors in Grimdean House were made from silver so they could trap evil spirits beneath the glass. Now the weird faces in the mirrors seemed even creepier than before.

The problem with Cryptorum's Chime lessons was that I'd always start daydreaming and the stuff he was telling us would trickle straight out of my head. I hoped none of it was life-saving information or I might be sorry one day – if we ever got to see a monster.

I dragged myself back upstairs behind Miss Smiting but when we reached the study no one was there.

"Robyn, we're in here." Aiden leant out of the next door along.

When I got inside, I understood exactly what Aiden had been up to for the past week. The flowery sofas had been pushed against the walls and three school desks had been put together in the centre of the room to make a workbench. The bench was scattered with tools and pieces of sawn wood, and a metal vice was fixed to the edge. Cryptorum's pet – the little crab creature with the eye on its shell – was wandering along the table. Every few steps it would stop and tilt its shell, as if peering round the room.

Nora was perched on the window sill, leafing through a book with a brown leather cover and yellowing pages. Cryptorum was striding up and down the room, muttering darkly.

"I didn't want to show you this until I knew it would work." Aiden picked up a long bow made from dark wood. "I've used toughened polymer for the bowstring. It'll shoot further now. And I've changed the shape to make the aim better too."

"Wow, you've been busy!" I admired the new bow.

Aiden grinned.

"Wait till you see the new swords." Nora closed her book with a snap, sending a tiny cloud of dust into the air. She sneezed, her plaits shaking.

"What have you done to the ssswords, Aiden?" Miss Smiting asked.

"I thought we needed a way of disguising them. That way we can carry them around all the time without people getting suspicious." Aiden picked up a long, metallic torch. "And the blade was so thin that I reckoned it could be folded into two sections. It took me hours to get it right but now it clicks open a bit like an umbrella. I'm calling it a torchblade."

"Let me show them!" Nora picked up a second torch and pressed a button on the handle. The metal casing clicked open and the sword sprang upwards, the silver blade gleaming.

"Awesome!" I stared at the sword. I could see a faint line halfway along where one part of the blade slipped inside the other like a telescope. "It's a genius idea. Does the torch bit light up as well?"

"Not yet, but I'm working on it." Aiden put down the torchblade and dusted off his hands. The huge smile on his face showed how pleased he was with what he'd made.

Cryptorum stopped pacing. "It's a ridiculous invention! Chime weapons have always been wood and silver – completely simple and straightforward. There's no need to try and modernize things. I didn't need a sword that disappeared inside a torch when I started fighting monsters!"

Aiden's face dropped. "I know it's not perfect yet but we need a way to disguise the blades when we go out."

Cryptorum waved his hand. "I suppose that part makes sense . . . but the ultrasonic blades and the subthermal scanners! There's a reason I never went in for any of that. It dulls all the instincts a Chime should be developing."

Subthermal *what*? I had no idea what Cryptorum was talking about but I was pretty mad at him for being mean after Aiden had worked so hard. "What's wrong with making something better? The monsters won't care what the weapons look like."

Miss Smiting hissed. "Robyn! Remember your mannerss."

Nora glanced worriedly from me to Cryptorum.

"Do you realize how little you know about being a Chime, young lady?" Cryptorum thundered. "There are creatures out there that can freeze your blood, but you can hardly concentrate long enough for me to tell you about them." Eye jumped, scuttled down the nearest table leg and hid under a sofa.

"Erasmusss, do be calm!" Miss Smiting urged.

I flushed. So he'd noticed my daydreaming. Aiden was giving me a *shut up* look, but I still couldn't stop myself saying, "Maybe we'd learn faster if you actually let us meet some monsters."

There was a long silence.

Cryptorum stomped over to the window. Darkness was gathering and an icy half-moon was rising over the trees at the end of the garden. "The bats have left." He turned to us, his eyes in shadow. "And I know exactly where they'll be. There's been trouble on Blagdurn Heath all week. Pick up your fancy torches and we'll go."

"Are you really letting us fight the creatures?" Nora went pale.

"Only if you want to." Cryptorum stomped to the door. "But she's right." He glared at me. "You won't learn to be a Chime by staying inside."

My eyes widened. Had he just admitted I was right? Was this some weird kind of test? I didn't care – I just wanted to get outside and fight something for real.

I grabbed a torchblade. Aiden picked up another and shoved it in his pocket. Then he slung his new bow over his shoulder and took a quiver of arrows. Nora picked up a torchblade too, and we followed Cryptorum to the front of Grimdean House where the shiny black limousine was parked.

Miss Smiting slid into the driver's seat while Cryptorum took the passenger's side and me, Aiden and Nora got into the back.

"Great – a Bat Club trip!" Aiden muttered.

I caught the sarcasm and noticed Nora's face looked even paler than usual. What had I got us into? Was this a really, REALLY bad idea? I was about to suggest going back inside when Miss Smiting stamped on the accelerator and the car jumped forward.

"Wait!" Nora gasped. "My mum will expect me home soon."

"I will ring your parents and tell them not to worry," Miss Smiting said. "I'll explain it's jussst a little field trip to study the nocturnal wildlife."

The limo zoomed up the street. I glimpsed the town square and then Ashbrook School with three huge tree trunks lying in the playground. Masses of scaffolding had gone up and there was a pile of bricks and roof tiles there too. I guessed the builders must be pretty busy. I remembered Aiden's doubts about the fallen trees. His suspicions didn't seem so weird any more.

"You don't know why those trees suddenly fell down on our school, do you?" I asked Cryptorum and Miss Smiting.

A slight smile curved Miss Smiting's lips as she glanced at me in the driving mirror.

"I hope you're not talking to me," Cryptorum growled. "My life was quiet and simple before you lot came along. Once in a while I'd get throttled by a scree sag or a kobold would bite me. But apart from all that, it was nice."

Nora gulped.

I tried to catch Miss Smiting's eye again but she wasn't looking. Surely she couldn't have knocked those trees down. She wouldn't be strong enough. Would she?

"I don't know how she did it but I bet those trees didn't fall down by themselves," Aiden whispered.

Orange street lamps whizzed past the car window. Then the streets turned to fields and we headed uphill. The limo banked sharply as we rounded a corner, throwing all of us to one side of the seat. A wilderness of bracken, muddy pools and stunted trees came into view, lit only by the half-moon. This was Blagdurn Heath, right on the edge of town. It was the nearest thing Wendleton had to a wasteland. I'd only come here once before – when Dad decided we should learn to put up a tent and cook on an open fire. We'd lasted half an hour. Annie had burnt her finger, I'd got a splinter and we'd driven back home buying burgers at the drive-through on the way.

Miss Smiting came to a halt beside a ditch. "Out you go!"

We sidled out. I looked round, trying to let my eyes get used to the dark.

Cryptorum popped the boot open and got out some ropes and a small metal cage. Miss Smiting handed us a toughened leather jacket each. This time they were more or less the right size. "I got these for you in town. They will protect you from the worssst bites and cuts. Have fun, darlings!"

She turned the limo round and screeched down the hill.

With ropes in one hand and the cage in the other, Cryptorum led us across the rough heath. The moon blinked out as a bank of dark clouds rolled across the sky and a freezing wind whistled through the bushes. The orange lights of Wendleton at the bottom of the hill seemed very far away.

A cluster of bats swooped in, filling the air with flapping sounds. Cryptorum waved them away and they clustered together and swarmed back towards town.

"Don't we need the bats to help us find things?" I asked.

"No, you should be more concerned with creatures finding *you*." Cryptorum sat on a large boulder and took a sandwich out of his pocket. "Go on then! I'll be over here if you need me."

"Huh?" I thought I'd heard him wrong.

"Like you said, you'll learn faster if you meet some monsters." He waved a hand to dismiss us. "So go – meet them! Take some rope if you like. Then you can bring back any creatures you catch. Don't fall off the cliff on the far side of the marsh. It's often hard to spot in the dark."

"Aren't you going to help us?" Nora asked.

"I've taught you a lot of the basics already. Miss Smiting will be back in an hour with the car. Try to return by then – and try not to get killed." He took a bite of his sandwich.

My face flamed. I was sure this was a trap. It was a way to scare us and make us admit we should do what he wanted – stay at Grimdean House and listen to him droning on the whole time. Or maybe he wanted to prove to Miss Smiting that he shouldn't train us at all. "Come on, guys," I said to Aiden and Nora. "Let's go."

Aiden picked up some rope and they followed me reluctantly. I found a sort-of path through the bracken. We passed the fallen tree trunk where my dad had tried to teach us how to light a fire and cook on it. My family would never believe what I was up to right now. I fiddled with my torch but instead of a beam of light the casing opened and the frostblade shot upwards. I'd forgotten that Aiden hadn't managed to get the light working yet.

We pushed our way through a tangle of bushes into a clearing. The half-moon came out, casting pale light across the heath. Leaves rustled. Branches cracked. Behind a stunted tree, something was moving. . .

Blagdurn Heath is Full of Nasty Surprises

id you see that?" Nora whispered. "Behind that tree."

"I saw it!" I pointed my blade at the tree. "Get your weapon out. We've got to be ready."

"No, just there!" Nora tugged my arm, nearly pulling me over.

She was right. There was something moving on the other side of the clearing. Surely they couldn't both be monsters – we couldn't be *that* unlucky. One of them had to be a squirrel or something.

"I'll take this one." Aiden dropped the rope and raised his bow, nocking an arrow into his bowstring. "Wait till they make a move."

I tried to keep my eyes fixed on the first creature

but I could see Nora struggling with the button on her torch. "Press it really hard and it'll open," I told her.

Clouds hid the moon and the clearing darkened. The rustling in the bushes grew louder. I strained my eyes, trying to see the creature.

"I just can't..." Nora pushed the button with both thumbs.

"Nora, come on!" I hissed.

"I'm trying. I think it's stuck."

I turned to help her just as she finally managed to release the button. Her torchblade sprang to life, knocking mine out of my hands. A sudden growling erupted on both sides of the clearing and a mass of creatures burst out of the bushes, slamming into Aiden and knocking his legs from under him. There were four of them, all half our size and covered in brown spines.

"Kobolds!" shouted Nora.

"I know! Get your sword!" I grabbed my blade and swung it like a baseball bat, forgetting every move Cryptorum had ever taught us. I wanted to catch one, take it back to Cryptorum and prove him wrong about everything, but I couldn't see the rope under the mass of spiny bodies. My heart thumped like crazy.

"Gah! Hit them, Rob!" Aiden said before getting buried below a sea of grunting spines.

I swung the sword again, striking one of the kobolds this time, but its hide was so tough that the blade just bounced off. I tried again but Nora got in the way and I missed. The little monsters growled and disappeared into the bushes. Aiden struggled up, grabbing his bow. "Let's get out of here."

We legged it, pushing through the trees and stumbling across an open stretch of heath dotted with watery ditches.

"Are you sure you're OK?" I said to Aiden.

"I'm fine. Mean little things, aren't they?" He rubbed his hair and loads of leaves fell out. His face was covered in scratches. "This was a bad idea, though. If you think about it we've only been training for a few days. We're just not good enough to be out here on our own." He glanced at Nora who was trying to pull off some ivy that'd got tangled round her sword.

"It's my fault Cryptorum brought us. I'm really sorry!" I pulled a face. "I reckon he's expecting us to run back to him and beg to be taken home. Let's at least hang around here for a while or he'll think we're useless."

"All right, but I'm seriously wondering if Bat Club

is turning out to be a big pain," Aiden frowned. "Making these weapons was fun, but Cryptorum didn't even like them. It's not like he wanted to share all this in the first place. He still wishes he was the only Chime in Wendleton."

Sometimes Aiden says wise stuff like that. I hoped he wouldn't give up on being a Chime though. I wasn't ready to quit and it would be WAY less fun without him.

"It's not working because of me," Nora said miserably. "I'm no good at this."

"Don't be silly – you're great," I said, nudging Aiden. I just hoped Nora wouldn't get in the way the next time a creature appeared.

"Yeah, you're fine," Aiden said, not very convincingly. "Maybe it would be better if you took the bow and arrows instead of that sword?"

Nora looked a bit downcast, but she swapped weapons with Aiden without complaining.

I suddenly wondered why I hadn't shivered when the monsters appeared. "I always used to shiver when there was a creature around but I don't any more," I told the others. "Did you guys have that?"

"Yeah." Aiden said.

"The *Journal of an Eighteenth Century Chime* by Edwin Crunstall says that shivering or trembling in the presence of a monster occurs when a person's Chime abilities have recently manifested. But the shivering generally only lasts for a short time," Nora told me. "Crunstall writes that he only noticed it for two weeks."

"Oh!" I said.

We trudged on, keeping to open areas and avoiding patches of trees and brambles where more kobolds might be hiding. The muddy pools scattered over this part of the heath became wider and deeper. In some places we had to jump to get across. Nora wobbled as she leapt over a pool and for a second I thought she was going to fall in head first.

"At least the kobolds can't follow us here," I said. "I don't think they'd get over these ditches with their short legs. What other monsters can we look for?"

"We're far away from people so probably vodanoys and grodders," Nora told me. "We might see an etting or a scree sag but bogguns mostly prefer staying in towns. I think we're too far south for a draka demon—"

"Hold it!" I jumped another ditch. "What are those creatures you said first?"

"Vodanoys and grodders, you mean?" Nora

followed me, grabbing my arm to keep her balance.

"I remember something about grodders," Aiden said. "Aren't they the big hairy bulls with the fiery red eyes?"

"Yeah. They can kill people by trampling them with their hooves. They're not very intelligent though," Nora added. "Sometimes other creatures will use them for pulling or carrying heavy things. The most famous grodder was the one belonging to the dark enchanter, Geraddin of France, who used to tie his enemies to its legs and have them dragged along. . ."

"Sounds like a nice guy." I was starting to wonder if Nora had memorized all of Cryptorum's books. "Anyway at least if the monster is big we'll see it coming. I seriously don't think there's anything here except those kobolds. Look – the whole place is empty." I waved my arm at the scrubby wasteland. "There's nothing here at all." I leapt across the next ditch. I was halfway over when something grabbed my ankle.

"Robyn!" cried Nora.

I fell and my sword tumbled out of my hand. The grip on my ankle got stronger, pulling me into the water. Twisting round, I kicked out with my other leg. My foot met something hard and the creature yelped.

I landed half in and half out of the muddy water and groped around for my sword. Now I could see the monster – a skinny creature with grey, clammy skin. Its hands were webbed but the freakiest things were its round bug-like eyes, flappy gills and fish-like mouth. It crept towards me, its mouth opening and closing.

I edged backwards, panic shooting up my spine.

"Hey!" Aiden leapt over, waving his sword. "Get back, you!"

The creature hissed and slid beneath the water till only its eyes and the top of its head were visible.

"Where's my sword?" I found the blade and staggered to the top of the bank.

The creature glided closer, its eyes still fixed on me.

"It's a vodanoy. They're like watery cousins of the kobolds," Nora whispered. "They like to drag people under the water."

"And how about that one?" I pointed my blade at the pale monster with masses of writhing tentacles and a jaw full of spiky teeth that was rising from the ditch behind her.

Nora and Aiden swung round. "It's a nesha!" squeaked Nora.

I started jumping ditches. I couldn't understand

131

why Aiden and Nora weren't moving. The nesha creature was still rising from the water and looking bigger and hungrier by the second. "Guys, wake up!"

Aiden jerked forward and they both ran. We didn't stop until we were far away from the ditches. I leant over, trying to get my breath back.

"On second thoughts," puffed Aiden. "I think I prefer the kobolds, so let's stay away from the water."

Nora had gone green. I hoped she wasn't going to pass out. "That nesha looked much worse than the picture in the book!"

"Probably because pictures in books can't jump out of the water and eat you," I said. "Hey, where's the bow?"

She flushed. "I must have dropped it. Sorry."

A horrible guilty feeling bubbled inside me. I was the one who had told Cryptorum to let us face real creatures. The others were obviously hating this and it was all my fault. "We should go back," I said. "Maybe it's time for Miss Smiting to collect us."

We made our way back through the bushes and patches of brambles and took a couple of wrong turns. There were no real paths on the heath and it was hard to work out where we were in the dark. At last we got to the log where my dad had tried to teach us how to cook on a fire and I knew we must be close to where we'd left Cryptorum.

I took a deep breath. I knew he was going to be smug. I guess I had to admit he was right – we had a lot more to learn.

We pushed our way through a gorse bush and the boulder was right up ahead. Cryptorum wasn't there. The cage he'd brought wasn't there either. I walked a bit further but I still couldn't see him.

"Mr Cryptorum?" Aiden called.

I checked my watch. "We've been more than an hour."

"He wouldn't have gone without us, would he?" Nora bit her lip. "I can't believe he'd do that."

I wasn't sure what Cryptorum would do. He was a guy who'd been fighting these unseen creatures nearly all his life. Maybe it had turned him a bit funny. "Why don't we look over here?" I pointed to a cluster of straggly trees. "We haven't been that way yet. If he's not close by we'll come back."

We walked through the trees, keeping really quiet. The only thing I could hear was the sound of our footsteps and the silence was starting to get on my nerves.

"I think we should go back," I said.

"Let's call him again." Nora opened her mouth but I grabbed her arm before she could yell.

"I don't think we should." I couldn't explain why. I just had the feeling that nasty things might hear us. "I really think we should go back. We're never gonna find—" I stopped, spotting a big, dark square through a gap in the trees. It was a really old, broken-down house. I didn't remember there being any houses on Blagdurn Heath. "Where did that come from?"

The moon sailed out from behind a cloud and the house suddenly looked extra creepy. The windows gaped where the glass should've been and the broken chimney looked like a crooked finger pointing at the sky.

I swallowed. In a dark gap beside the wall, two red lights were burning.

No, not lights – two fiery red eyes. There was also a big hairy body shaped like a bull and the meanest pair of horns I'd ever seen. The beast pawed the ground with its hoof.

I felt Nora tense. "It's a grodder," she whispered. "Don't make a noise. You can't outrun them. They're really fast and really strong."

My blood was pounding in my ears. "Can't we just give it hay or something?"

We started to back up slowly. The beast didn't

move. We backed up some more. The grodder lifted its head and gave a huge bellow that rang out across the heath.

Then it charged.

Nora Knows Useful Facts About Hairy Monster Bulls

he fiery red eyes burned into us. The grodder's hooves thundered on the dry ground.

"Run!" I yelled. Branches snatched at my hair as I sprinted through the trees.

Nora stumbled and I grabbed her arm, pulling her up. The monster had reached the thicket. Gaining speed, it smashed through trees as if they weren't even there. It was even bigger than I'd first thought – as big as a car – and its horns stretched into two very nasty points. It bellowed again and the drumming of its hooves grew faster.

Nora looked back and gave a little shriek.

Aiden veered off to the right. "Split up!" he shouted. "Maybe it'll get confused."

"He's right!" I gasped.

Nora ran left. I slowed a little, trying to see which way the grodder would go. The beast tossed its head and charged me. I ran faster than I'd ever run before. My legs burned – filled with panicked energy. This was good – the monster had left Aiden and Nora alone. But soon I was going to be grodder toast.

I looked back and wished I hadn't. Beneath its red eyes, the beast had two huge nostrils and I was close enough to see the forest of hairs inside them. The monster pitched its head, probably in anticipation of tossing me into the air on its spiky horns.

Suddenly a loud snorting sound came from the left. Was that Nora? She sounded really strange and I thought for a second she must be hurt.

"Moo-eee-ohhh!" she groaned.

The grodder slowed a little.

"Mooo-eee-ay-eee-ay-ohhh!" Nora went on.

The monster swung its head, searching for the sound. I dodged behind a tree trunk. "Nora, what are you doing?" I hissed.

She carried on with the weird noises. "Mooo-ohhh!"

The grodder stopped completely. It sniffed the

air, turning its head to and fro. Whatever Nora was doing, it was working. The beast took a few steps towards the noise and stopped again.

"Eee-ay-eee-ay-ohhh!" yelled Nora.

The grodder gambolled towards her, its steps almost dainty. I leant against the tree, hoping it wouldn't hear me trying to catch my breath. Peeking round the tree trunk, I watched the creature stop and swing its head from side to side. "Moo-ohh?" it groaned, trotting along again with its tail twirling happily.

I stared. What was going on?

Aiden broke through the trees. "Don't stop!" he hissed. "That thing could turn mean any second."

I raced after him and we didn't stop running until we were far away from the thicket and those bright red eyes.

"Where's Nora?" I scanned the darkness. "If she got caught by that beast—"

"I'm here!" Nora dashed round a bramble patch. Her plaits had unravelled and there was mud all over her face. "I think I've lost it. That was really close!"

"What were you doing?" I said. "Do you speak monster bull language or something?"

"It was a grodder mating call," Nora told me. "I read about it in one of Cryptorum's books – about the quadrupeds of the Unseen World. Actually I used the female mating call, which was a bit risky because if that one had been a girl then it would've thought its territory was being stolen and would've turned even meaner."

I stared at her. "The grodder was a boy?"

"It must have been," she agreed.

"A boy grodder looking for a girlfriend?" I grinned.

Nora wiped her forehead. "Yeah! I think it was pretty desperate for love judging by the loudness of its mooing."

I snorted with laughter.

"That was a really good idea." Aiden told her.

"Good idea?" I said. "That was a-MAZ-ing! That thing would have trampled me if it hadn't been for you."

Nora went pink. "Thanks! It was lucky I'd read that book. . ."

"You totally kept your cool too. It was seriously impressive." This was big praise from Aiden so Nora went even pinker. Aiden tested the opening and closing of his torchblade. "The new swords worked pretty well too."

A car horn beeped in the distance. "I really hope that's Miss Smiting."

We hurried in the direction of the sound. So we

hadn't actually caught anything, but at least we'd faced some creatures and survived. We were a pretty good team too. Aiden had made us weapons and Nora knew useful stuff. And me – well, I wasn't bad with a sword.

The black limo was waiting next to the ditch again. I'd never been so happy to see a car before.

"I promisssed your parents I would bring you home," Miss Smiting said as we climbed in "Did you have fun?"

Fun. That was one word for it.

"Er, kind of," Aiden replied. "What happened to Mr Cryptorum?"

"He returned early after catching three kobolds." Miss Smiting accelerated down the hill. "The batsss found signs of creature activity elsewhere. You know that the bats help Erasmus – they are able to sssense things. Dark things."

We nodded.

"So he left to invessstigate." Miss Smiting turned the limo sharply and screeched to a halt outside my house.

I went inside, glancing into the hall mirror as I took off my shoes. There were leaves in my hair and a scratch all the way across my face where a tree branch had whipped me.

"There you are!" Mum came in. "You look like you've been at a war, not a nature club. That Miss Smiting said the trip was to Blagdurn Heath, so what on earth did you find up there in the dark?"

"Um ... nothing much... I think I saw a squirrel," I said vaguely, shoving the torch with its hidden blade deeper into my pocket. "What's for tea?"

Cryptorum didn't return to Grimdean House that week and Miss Smiting told us nothing about where he'd gone. She was pretty busy keeping our school running and Mrs Lovell seemed happy for her to do it. She had a ramp installed by the front steps for the boy two years below who used a wheelchair. She organized a proper music stand for Miss Mason, and asked Mr Paggley to always serve pizza and ice cream on Fridays as a treat for the kids.

She was pretty popular with everyone.

Bat Club wasn't the same without Cryptorum. Miss Smiting told us she couldn't train us in combat although she let us practise against each other. Aiden settled down to perfect the torchblades and soon both blade and torch parts were working perfectly. Nora read more books and practised archery with me until she was hitting the bullseye just as often as I was. Even Aiden admitted privately that she was now a pretty essential member of our team.

On the Monday after our trip to the heath, we were hanging out upstairs in Cryptorum's study after school. Miss Smiting was in a chatty mood so I asked her how much she liked moving to Wendleton after living in a rainforest.

"It iss a little hard to remember. It wass fifty years ago, you understand, but I do remember that we arrived here in winter. I had never realized a place could be sso terribly cold." She shivered at the thought.

"Why did you come?" I asked.

"My dear, Erassmus had saved my life. He fought off the two-headed wraith-gator which had sstalked me for many months." Her green eyes flickered. "So I came here to assist him for a while and I have never looked back."

"So Mr Cryptorum was already fighting monsters by then?" Aiden asked.

"He wasss. But he had been away from this town for yearsss and the place had become overrun by vampires. They gathered in the town square at night and prowled the streetsss attacking anyone who ventured out. The people blamed warring gangs – they did not understand the danger." Miss

Smiting rose from her armchair and drifted over to the window. "The leader called herself Pearl – a vampire of such power that she was able to go out in the ssunlight."

"Not many of them can do that," Nora put in.

"She walked the streetss in her gaudy clothes and her boots studded with rhinestones, looking for new victimss. The horrid creature seemed to think she was ssome kind of celebrity." Miss Smiting ended with a sharp hiss. "Her boldnesss gave other nasty creatures the confidence to roam around the town too."

I tried to imagine crowds of monsters wandering freely around Wendleton with most people totally unaware. It was bad enough to have a few kobolds appearing in our garden. "People couldn't see the vampires though, could they?" I asked. "They're just another kind of monster."

"Vampires are not like other monsterss," Miss Smiting said. "They walk in both the human and the Unseen worldss. Most of the time, they look like any normal person you might pass on the street. So yess, people would have seen them but they would not have understood the peril."

"It must have been so scary." Nora clasped her hands together. "And Cryptorum had to fight them all alone."

"It was not easy, but he was younger then." Miss Smiting glanced at the photo on the desk showing Cryptorum with no lines on his face, his hair brown instead of grey. "He had the . . . what isss it called? The youthful energy."

"That's why you wanted him to find more Chimes like us, isn't it? Because he's getting older." Aiden studied Miss Smiting intently. "Was it you who made the trees fall on top of our old school so that we'd have to move in here? How did you do it?"

Miss Smiting smiled. "Ah, that was not difficult. Where I come from there is a special moth – the moondust moth – which has spotted white wings. They love to eat roots so I sssimply released them into little holes beside the trees."

"Wasn't that dangerous?" Nora's eyes widened.

"Not at all! I gave the moths time to work and then returned one night to give the trees a final push in the right direction."

Aiden and I exchanged looks. He had a satisfied expression on his face. I knew he'd always suspected the trees hadn't fallen down on their own.

"Now we musst get on." Miss Smiting continued briskly. "I have a special task for you today. Using ice-cream tubs we will make some little hibernation homes for the winter animalss."

"But we need to practise our Chime skills!" I couldn't believe it. I hadn't stayed late to play with ice-cream tubs.

"It's probably because of me." Nora turned pink. "My mum told me she was going to phone Mrs Lovell and talk about how much time I was spending at Bat Club. She said she wasn't sure it was a suitable kind of club. She and my dad are both teachers at the high school and she wants me to get home earlier so she can help me with my homework."

I pulled a sympathetic face. Nora had told me the other day that she didn't have any brothers or sisters. That sounded awesome to me but maybe it wasn't as great as I thought. I couldn't imagine my parents insisting on doing homework with me.

"So we will do ssome nice things." Miss Smiting picked up a bag of bits and pieces she'd left by the door. "Houses for mouses and maybe a bird table. Then before you go home, I will let you borrow a book from Erasmus's collection so that you can study Chime skills a little more."

"Ooh, great!" Nora's eyes lit up. "I know exactly which book I want to take."

A clattering sound came from downstairs.

Miss Smiting's tongue flickered as if she was tasting the air. "Dratted children! They are trying to ssneak around again." She handed the bag of stuff to Aiden. "Take these things next door and get started. I will deal with the little monkeyss. Robyn, fetch the sticky tape from Mr Cryptorum's cupboard. I will return in a moment." With a swish of her skirts, she zipped from the room.

"I bet it's Hector again," Aiden said. "He can't stand the idea that we've been chosen for this club and he hasn't."

"If he knew we were making mouse houses from ice-cream tubs he might not be so jealous." I bent down to open the cupboard but it was stuck. "Did she mean this cupboard? Guys?" I straightened up to find that Aiden and Nora had already gone next door. Sighing, I tried the cupboard again. Then I tried the desk drawers. There were pens and a rusty old key, but no sign of sticky tape. I scanned the room.

My eyes fell on a little white cupboard between the painting of Cryptorum's parents and the bookcase. It was the same colour as the wall, which made it easy to overlook. When I found it was locked, I fetched the key I'd seen in the drawer. The key turned and the door swung open.

Inside there was a small glass box – like a tiny fish tank. Floating inside the tank was a pale green bubble, its shiny surface flecked with purple. I knew straight away what it was – a wish.

As I watched the wish bubble began to move faster, bumping against the sides and the top of the tank like a bird that wanted to be free. I leant in, trying to look at the picture inside the wish, but it was hard to see. Why did Cryptorum keep a wish trapped in here? What was so special about it?

I spotted a photo frame lying flat on the shelf above and picked it up. I recognized the smiling woman with curly brown hair in the picture. I'd seen her in another of Cryptorum's photos. She was wearing a woollen hat and her cheeks were shiny and red.

Aiden came back. "Robyn, what are you doing? You're missing all the mouse house fun."

Nora was right behind him. "I made a little mouse door knocker on my tub. You've got to come and see it!"

"Guys, look at this." I showed them the photo. "There's a wish trapped in here and I reckon this is the same lady as the one in the other photo. Do you think the wish is about her?"

Nora picked up the photo from Cryptorum's desk and held the pictures side by side. In the second photo the lady was pictured with Cryptorum and Miss Smiting. "It's definitely the same person."

The wish bumped against the side of the glass. In the middle of the gleaming bubble, I thought I glimpsed Cryptorum's face.

"Chimes! What have you *done*?" Miss Smiting whipped across the room and took the photos away from us. Her eyes flashed. "Why are you going through these cupboardss? Explain yourself!"

"I was trying to find the sticky tape like you said." My stomach plunged. "I wasn't trying to snoop, honest!"

"Thiss cupboard is private." Miss Smiting replaced the photos where they belonged.

"Why is that wish trapped in a box?" I tried to get another look but she closed the door and locked it firmly.

"Because that'ss the best place for it," she snapped. "Do not mention what you've seen to anyone. No one knows about the wish except for those who are close to Erasmus."

"We won't say anything. We promise!" Nora said.

"But who's that lady in the picture?" I couldn't help asking.

Miss Smiting studied me with a stern look in her green eyes. "That was Rebecca, Erasmus's wife, and the case containss her very last wish before she died. You must never, *ever* touch it."

Something Unexpected Lands on the Grimdean Lawn

An icy wind was pulling the last leaves off the trees as I walked to Grimdean House the next morning. The shops in town had started putting up Christmas decorations in their windows. I knew Mr Cryptorum was back as soon as I heard his deep voice complaining to Miss Smiting. "So many children! I'd forgotten how loud they are. And where's Eye? You can hardly blame her for hiding from this commotion."

Mrs Lovell announced in assembly that the damage to Ashbrook School was worse than everyone had expected. "It looks as if something gnawed the roots and caused the trees to fall down," she explained. "Although I don't know of any creature that could do that! But the building still needs a lot of repair work so we could be at Grimdean House for many weeks yet."

None of the kids seemed bothered by this. In a strange sort of way, being at Grimdean had started to feel normal. The assembly finished with "Rudolph the Red-Nosed Reindeer" played on the recorder by two girls in Nora's class.

Annie had been going on about the recorder at home. Miss Mason had offered to give lessons to some of the little kids and they all went to a recorder group on Monday lunchtimes. The squeaky sounds drifted down the corridors, driving everyone mad. Annie had pestered Mum and Dad until they gave in and paid for the recorder lessons, and now she wanted to put on "concerts" in the living room all the time. Still, that was the least of my problems.

I was desperate to know what that wish trapped in the glass case was all about.

"I'm going to ask Cryptorum," I said to Aiden as we ran outside for Bat Club after school. "And I'll ask him why he's been gone so long too."

Aiden zipped up his jacket. "Don't! You'll only make him mad."

Nora was already down by the shed helping

Cryptorum take out equipment ready for our training session.

Cryptorum leant a bow against the shed wall. "We'll start with a reminder of the basics," he said to us. "Swords then bows."

"Um ... sir?" I said. "Can I ask you something?"

"What's that?" Cryptorum dumped a quiver of arrows on the ground.

I went cold. I'd forgotten how fierce he looked. His eyebrows seemed even thicker than before. "Er ... I just wondered what monsters you found while you were away."

"There's no time for that." Cryptorum gave a frostblade to each of us. Aiden had taken our torchblades back so he could check how they were working. "Right, show me your defence position."

I gripped my blade tightly. Why did he have to keep everything a secret? We were Chimes too. "But we'll be facing monsters soon, won't we? So we need to know what's out there."

"That depends on how much progress you make." Cryptorum fixed me with a glare. "I'm not letting you run around Wendleton if you don't know what you're doing. Now show me your defence position."

Gritting my teeth, I got into position – legs

shoulder-width apart, knees slightly bent and two hands holding the blade.

"Now show me your side swipe and over-the-head attack moves," Cryptorum growled. "Give yourself more space, Nora, or you'll skewer Aiden."

I did the side-swipe move. I'd got this stuff right ages ago. When were we going to do something new? A buzzing grew and grew inside my head. I thought it was me getting annoyed, but then a bright light swept over us and the rhythmic chopping and droning got even louder.

"Get back!" Cryptorum's voice was almost drowned out by the noise of the helicopter. He grabbed Nora who was gaping at the sky.

We backed up towards the shed. The helicopter landed halfway down the lawn and the rotating blades spun slowly to a stop. The pilot jumped down and helped a man in a dark suit from the back of the helicopter. The man had black hair greying a little at the sides and a lean face with watchful eyes that made me think of a leopard. He rested on his silver-topped cane and studied us, smiling. "Erasmus! I couldn't resist popping in."

"Dominic." Cryptorum frowned. "My neighbours tend to complain when you land here. They hate the noise of that thing."

The visitor waved the objection away. "Oh, we shan't disturb you for long."

Three figures dressed in black leapt out of the helicopter behind him. The tallest was a blond-haired boy around a year or two older than me and Aiden. There was also a girl with a sleek, dark ponytail and a thin boy with a pale face. They each held a slim metal cylinder and their black leather jackets fitted them perfectly – nothing like the chunky ones that Miss Smiting had bought us. On their wrists, they wore identical black watches with curved screens that looked pretty expensive.

"Robyn, Aiden, Nora." Cryptorum turned to us. "This is Mr Dray. He's a Chime and a long-time friend and associate. I visited his home, Kesterly Manor, while I was gone."

"So these are the trainees." Mr Dray's gaze swept over us, lingering on our badly fitting jackets and bare frostblades. His smile widened. "I wanted to bring my own apprentices to meet you. It's so important to make connections, isn't it? This is Rufus." He pointed to the tall blond boy. "And Portia and Tristan."

"Hi!" Nora said excitedly. "I didn't realize other Chimes were training nearby. It's so great to meet you."

"Yeah." Portia rolled her eyes and I felt myself redden on Nora's behalf. I didn't like that girl's attitude and I didn't like the smug way the blond boy was looking at us either.

Mr Dray waved his silver-topped cane towards the house. "Let us go in, Erasmus. I have gathered further information since last week relating to the vampire activity in the north. We'll leave the youngsters to get acquainted. I'm sure they'll have a lot to teach each other." He called to the pilot. "Come inside, Sanders."

Cryptorum locked the door to the weapons shed before following Mr Dray. "I won't be long," he told us.

As the adults disappeared inside, I stared doubtfully at the three new kids. They looked way too perfect in those leather jackets and what were those cylinders they were holding? I didn't want to ask and look stupid.

Aiden broke the silence. "So you're training as Chimes too."

"Well, Mr Dray belongs to the International Federation of Chimes," Portia told us. "And once we've earned our certificate we will too."

I exchanged looks with Aiden. There was a certificate?

Rufus laughed. "Didn't you realize there are

Chimes all over the world and new ways of killing monsters? Cryptorum's a bit stuck in the past, isn't he? It must be really annoying."

I scowled. *He* was really annoying. "Have you been training for long then?"

"Since I was four," Rufus said. "You?"

Portia smirked. "They've been training for a few weeks, remember? Mr Dray told us."

"How did you train at age four?" I said. "Did you really have Chime powers that young?"

"Course we did!" Rufus said. "We got our abilities when Mr Dray had a Mortal Clock fitted to the Kesterly town hall. He says he knew there would be talented Chimes like us in the town."

I wanted to ask them what creatures they'd faced so far but I had a horrible feeling they'd seen a lot more action than Aiden, Nora and me.

"Luckily for us Mr Dray's equipped Kesterly Manor with masses of training equipment." Rufus went on, pushing back his blond fringe. "There's a climbing wall, environmental controls so that we can practise in different weather conditions – oh, and awesome gear." He pressed a button on the metal cylinder in his hand and a pale gold blade leapt into the air. If you looked closely the metal seemed to be moving all the time like water pouring from a tap. I must've looked surprised because he grinned. "Ultrasonic blade, see!"

"Oh!" Nora gasped. "You mean it uses sound waves to disrupt a monster's life force? That's ... um. . ." She tailed off as she caught my glare.

Rufus carried on. "And our watches monitor our vital signs – heart rate, oxygen level, stuff like that – so Mr Dray can check our health when we're fighting hostile creatures." He held out his arm and the screen on his watch lit up, flashing different numbers as he pressed the display. "Cool, isn't it?"

"Sure the sword looks pretty," I said. "But how fast can you beat a monster with it?"

"Let's have a competition and find out." Rufus turned. "Trist, get the subthermal scanners and meta-tensile rope out of the helicopter. Whoever catches a creature first is the winner. Doesn't matter if it's dead or alive."

"Robyn, we can't. . ." Aiden muttered.

Aiden was right. We couldn't leave the Grimdean garden or Cryptorum would kill us, but I didn't want to tell these kids that. "Why don't we fight instead?" I held out my sword. "Me against you."

"Sure! If you think you can handle it." Rufus began circling me, his gold blade shimmering. I wondered if it hurt more to be hit by one of those things than a normal sword. I had a feeling I was about to find out.

"Wait!" Nora jumped between us just as I aimed a side swipe at Rufus. I had to throw myself backwards to avoid hitting her. Losing my balance, I fell over and dropped my sword. Portia snickered.

"Look at the bats – they've sensed something!" Nora pointed to the stream of dark shapes pouring from the barn.

"The subthermal scanner's picked something up too." Tristan was holding a small grey box covered with flickering red and green lights.

"I'll notify Mr Dray." Portia turned towards the house but Cryptorum and Dray were already coming.

"Dear, dear, I hope any duels were amicable." Mr Dray looked from the mud smears on my jacket to the frostblade I'd dropped on the ground. "You can't expect such recently recruited trainees to be a match for my Beast Undercover Tracking Taskforce."

Cryptorum's eyes flashed. "Robyn, Aiden and Nora make a good team and they're a match for anybody. Now, if you don't mind." He glanced at the bats wheeling through the darkening sky.

I flushed. *A match for anybody.* It was the first time Cryptorum had said anything nice about us.

"It was a pleasure to see you, Erasmus." Mr Dray

nodded, before letting the pilot help him back into the helicopter.

"Maybe we'll finish that fight another time." Rufus twirled his ultrasonic blade.

"Fine by me!" I said.

"I'm surprised he can fit his head inside that helicopter," Nora muttered as we watched them climb aboard.

I smiled. Nora was always so nice – it was funny to hear her say something mean.

"Beast Undercover Tracking Taskforce," Aiden repeated. "That's great when you shorten it."

"BUTT!" I nearly collapsed with laughter.

We stood back as the propellers started to spin and the helicopter rose in a whirl of dust and noise. At last it flew off into the dark.

Cryptorum stared at us from under lowered eyebrows. "Don't be distracted by Mr Dray and his fancy devices. Being a Chime isn't about flashy blades and silly gadgets. That's enough for this evening – head home, the three of you."

Before we left, Aiden gave us our torchblades back. I flicked the switch and the torch glowed. No one would ever guess that there was a sword hidden inside. It may not have been an ultrasonic blade, but

Aiden had made it himself. I bet none of the BUTT kids could actually invent stuff.

As we turned a corner, something reared up in front of us. I leapt into action, my hand on my torchblade. The wind gusted and the white thing fluttered away – just a piece of paper caught against a drainpipe. My shoulders slumped.

"You're jumpy today," Aiden said.

"Don't you think Cryptorum should have taken us with him?" I said.

Aiden gave me a look. "Is this about the BUTT squad?"

I grinned. Aiden knows me pretty well. "It's not just that. Cryptorum wants us to practise but apart from that one time on Blagdurn Heath we haven't actually done any monster fighting."

"Cryptorum's not going to let us out just because you want him to." He turned into his road. "See you tomorrow."

I knew Aiden was right. Cryptorum wasn't going to do anything he didn't want to. He hadn't even told us about the International Federation of Chimes. I couldn't stop thinking about the wish in his cupboard too. It seemed such a weird thing to do – to keep a dead person's wish. It did belong to his wife, I suppose, but I still found it creepy.

What did people wish for before they died, anyway? I'd checked the cupboard before Bat Club but it was locked and the key wasn't in the desk drawer any more.

Cryptorum definitely liked keeping secrets, but now I had one of my own.

Last week, Miss Smiting had told us we could borrow one book each from Cryptorum's study as long as we didn't show it to anyone and brought it back before the holidays. She'd nodded approvingly when I'd chosen *Advanced Moves With a Frostblade*, which had instructions about sword moves inside and looked super-useful. She'd turned to help Aiden – who wanted something with tons of diagrams because of his dyslexia – so she hadn't seen me slip a smaller book called *Wishes and Mysteries* inside the bigger one. It had a picture of floating wishes etched across the front cover. I'd spotted this book earlier and I was curious about what was inside.

I promised myself I'd put it back safely once I was done. Both books were in my rucksack, wrapped inside the raincoat that Mum had made me take to school.

"Hey, spacy!" Ben, who'd just got off the bus, caught up with me as I went down the path to the kitchen door. "So how's life at the House of Grim?"

I shrugged. "It's all right."

The kitchen was a wall of noise and steam. Annie and Josh were in a tug of war over a colouring pen.

I dashed upstairs. I wanted to figure out somewhere really good to hide Cryptorum's books while Annie wasn't in the room. She had a knack for discovering things you didn't want her to find. I stashed them under my bed and pushed them right to the back. I was just about to open my torchblade and try out some moves when Annie burst in, recorder in hand.

"Can I play you my new song?" She made her eyes big and round like she always does when she wants something.

"Um, I can't right now." I edged to the door. "You stay here and play your recorder. I'll leave you to it." I fled to the bathroom and locked the door. At last I was by myself. Maybe here I could practise sword moves in peace. I pressed the torch button and the blade sprang free.

Bang! Bang! Someone thumped on the bathroom door.

"Who's in there?" Sammie called. "Get out! I need to use the bathroom."

"Go away! I was here first," I yelled back.

Sammie stomped away, muttering. Honestly, there were just too many people in this house.

I held up the frostblade and tried to focus. What were the three Rs of sword play? Be *ready*, assess *risk*, then *react*. Cryptorum had repeated that over and over. The main risk was Sammie wanting the bathroom. That and the really hairy spider that was lurking on the ceiling.

I swished the blade lightly then I went through the basic moves – blocking and thrusting – before trying some of the fancy stuff. The silver blade gleamed in the bathroom light as I started getting into a rhythm. Those kids with their helicopter thought they were so awesome, but I bet we were just as good as them.

Bang! Bang!

The noise made me jump and I lost my balance, slicing the shower curtain that hung beside the bath.

"What are you *doing* in there?" Sammie said through the door.

"Mind your own business!" I quickly put away the blade and pushed the shower curtain back as far as it would go. Maybe if it was bunched up then no one would notice the massive rip for a while. I unlocked the door.

"Finally!" Sammie scowled. "Why did you

have to take so long? And what were those weird thumping noises you were making?"

"Go easy, Sammie!" Mum came past carrying a pile of towels. "You need to let people use the bathroom in peace."

Behind me the whole shower rail collapsed into the bath, taking the curtain with it.

"Oh, Robyn, did you have an accident?" Mum sighed. "Never mind. I'll see if your dad can fix it."

Sammie folded her arms and waited for me to pass, a huge smirk on her face.

My face flamed. It was all her fault. I'd been doing something important – practising sword skills that could save someone's life one day. I longed to tell them I was learning to fight deadly monsters but I knew I couldn't. Mum would think I was inventing the story and she might say I couldn't stay for Bat Club any more.

I pulled down my jumper to hide the torchblade bulge in my pocket. There was no way I would ever give up training. If that meant I had to keep my mouth shut – something I'd never been very good at – then that was the way it had to be.

I Trap a Kobold in a Roasting Dish

iss Smiting frowned when I asked if we could start fighting creatures like real Chimes. "Of course you can't! Don't be ssilly! Mr Cryptorum iss not here."

"But, miss!" I began, but she slipped up the stairs. The clock chimed and I knew it was time for school to start.

It had been three days since Mr Dray had landed his helicopter on the Grimdean lawn and we hadn't seen Cryptorum in all that time. He was still out monster-hunting while we were stuck here in lessons.

"She said no. I can't believe it!" I whispered to Aiden when I got to class. I'd told him my plan on the way to school. "She was the one that wanted Cryptorum to train us in the first place. Now she won't let us do anything!"

"We can still train after school," Aiden said. "What's the rush anyway? I've got a new prototype for an arrow I want to work on."

"I bet Rufus and those other kids get to fight real monsters." I looked up to check Mrs Perez wasn't listening. "And I bet we're just as good as them. We were fine on Blagdurn Heath."

"Yeah. Apart from the part where we nearly became a grodder's snack."

A deep moan came from the boggun in the dungeon below. It cut short suddenly. A moment later there was a scuffling sound from behind the wall, like a bunch of spiny kobold feet making a run for it. The noise passed on. I exchanged looks with Aiden.

"Robyn Silver, do you plan on daydreaming the whole lesson away?" Mrs Perez demanded.

"No, miss!" I bent over my book. As I tried to work, I felt something knocking against my ankle. Looking under the desk I found Eye tapping me with her claws. I kicked her off gently. What was she doing down here? I'd never seen her downstairs before.

"There's something under your chair," Sally-Anne hissed.

I tried to hide Eye with my feet. Could ordinary people see the little creature? If Sally-Anne got a good look at Eye she'd really have something to gossip about. "It's just a beetle," I muttered. "It's gone now."

Sally-Anne kept shooting looks at me and Eye kept tapping on my feet. Was the creature trying to tell me something?

The door was flung open and Annie stood there trembling. "Please, Mrs Perez! Miss Rawlings says can she have some help. Something's made a mess in our classroom."

I leapt to my feet, my heart racing. "Miss, I'm her sister. I'll go!"

"Sit down, Robyn." Mrs Perez frowned at me. "Hector, can you give Miss Rawlings a hand?"

"Yes, miss." Hector made a smug face.

I glared as I watched him go. I had a really bad feeling about this and I needed to get to Annie's classroom. My hands tightened on the edge of my desk.

A scream came from down the passageway. Ignoring Mrs Perez, I jumped up and sprinted from the room.

The ballroom was a complete mess. Trays of paint and paintbrushes were scattered everywhere, and little kids were running to and fro. A kobold, its feet covered in blue paint, was jumping from one table to another. The wall tapestry was bulging suspiciously. I ran over and shut the door to the hidden passage. If this kobold had escaped from the dungeon then what else was free?

"There must be a squirrel in here somewhere." Hector had a dazed look in his eyes. "A really big squirrel."

The kobold ran up the wall, leaving blue footprints everywhere. A shadow glided past me as I tracked the kobold. I glanced back but it was gone.

"Miss, if you take the kids out I'll get rid of the creature," I told Miss Rawlings. The teacher seemed as dazed as Hector, so I just yelled, "Extra break time!"

The little kids ran out of the door, cheering, and Miss Rawlings followed them. As soon as they'd gone, Aiden dashed in.

"Mrs Perez sent *me* down here." Hector's face reddened. "So you two can go away!"

The kobold ran to the middle of the ceiling and hung there, bristling and dripping blue paint. Some of it landed on Hector's head. He groped his hair, frowning. "There must be a leaky pipe."

"Get Nora and Miss Smiting," I muttered to Aiden. "Other monsters might be loose too. We need a way to get everyone out. . ."

"The fire alarm!" Aiden rushed off and a minute later the alarm started ringing.

Each class began filing out, thinking it was just a drill.

The kobold on the ceiling gave a menacing growl. Hector stood underneath, completely oblivious. "Robyn, get out of here! I don't need your help."

I bit my lip. I was so tempted to let the kobold bite Hector. It wouldn't kill him after all. I sighed. I had to be good. I was a Chime and I had a sacred duty – or whatever Cryptorum would've said. I touched the torchblade in my pocket. So how was I going to get rid of Hector?

The kobold gave me no time to think. It leapt from the ceiling, teeth gnashing.

"Hector, catch!" I seized a paint-splattered plastic table cover and threw it over his head. Then I opened my torchblade and slashed at the creature. The kobold growled and jumped out of an open window. I collapsed my sword just as Hector freed himself and Aiden and Nora ran in.

"I'm telling Mrs Perez what you did!" Hector stormed.

"Go tell her then!" I called after him. "I chased off your squirrel, by the way."

"I think Miss Smiting's gone out," Aiden puffed. "The limo's not there."

"I cornered a kobold in my classroom and locked it in a china cabinet," Nora said.

I looked at her with new respect. "So if all the creatures in the dungeon have escaped then what have we got left to catch?"

"One kobold, one boggun and a scree sag," Nora said. "But how did they get loose? There are so many doors and padlocks down there."

"Let's think about that afterwards." I drew my blade. "All I know is the door behind the tapestry was open. We've got to assume everything got out."

"We should split up – we'll cover more rooms that way," Aiden said.

"Right," I agreed. "Meet you back here. Have you got weapons?"

They both nodded. "Take one of these." Nora gave us a little hand mirror each. "It'll trap a boggun, but only for an hour or so because it's so small. The *Field Guide to Wraiths, Phantoms and Bogguns* says that if it's held close enough, a mirror

172

will attract a boggun and draw it in like a vacuum cleaner, and then—"

I patted her shoulder. "Tell me later, OK? It should work and that's good enough for me." I stuck the mirror in my spare pocket. "You guys go upstairs. I'll check things out down here."

I crept through the empty rooms, scanning the places a monster might hide – under grand pianos, behind velvet couches and in wooden cabinets. The school desks in each room were littered with pencils, rubbers and books left open as the kids ran out in a hurry.

I froze. I was sure I'd heard something. My heart started racing.

The noise came again – a cracking sound, like dry bones moving. A scree sag. A black-eyed face leered from behind the heavy curtains. With a high-pitched scream, the creature threw itself at me. The sound drilled into my brain and for a second I couldn't move. Bony fingers fastened on my shoulder and felt for my neck. I slashed with my sword but the creature grabbed my throat and squeezed.

I gasped for breath. The scree sag leant in, its lips stretched in a hideous grin. I kicked out with all my strength. The creature's leg bone crunched and it staggered backwards. Taking a gasping breath, I swung my sword.

The scree sag's ribs snapped and it crumpled into a heap.

I rubbed my neck, feeling pretty relieved. I was sure that no one except a Chime could see the scree sag's bones but I kicked them under a cabinet just in case.

Through the window, I could see the teachers lining up their classes on the lawn. Miss Mason was standing with Josh's class, her red-and-silver scarf flapping in the wind. Soon the teachers would count everyone and bring them back in but there was still another kobold and a boggun to find.

I checked out the rest of the downstairs, including all the rooms marked KEEP OUT. When I got to the kitchen, I found a kobold cramming cheesecake between its spiky teeth. It leapt on to the worktop, scattering dishes. Crumbs flew into the air.

I raised my torchblade. "If Nora was here she'd tell me your usual diet and I bet it's not cheesecake."

The kobold snarled.

"You've probably ruined the only nice pudding we'll get all week." I brought the sword down on its spiny head. The creature yelped but the blade bounced off. Kobold skin was so tough.

I struck again and the beast fell back into a huge roasting dish. I clapped the lid on and weighed it down with a sack of potatoes. If Miss Smiting came back soon, maybe she could bag this creature and take him to Blagdurn Heath where he could play with his pals. After all, kobolds weren't deadly, just not very human-friendly.

Two down. Now for the boggun.

I spun round, glimpsing a shadow from the corner of my eye. There it was – slipping through the doorway. Pulling the mirror from my pocket, I followed it down the corridor. I thought I'd lost it until I saw a shadow sliding up the stairs. Jumping over the KEEP OUT sign I ran after it and nearly crashed into Aiden and Nora at the top.

"I've killed the scree sag and the kobold's stuck in the kitchen," I panted. "Just got to get this boggun." I looked round but the boggun had gone.

Nora stared. "We've already caught the boggun. Aiden trapped it five minutes ago."

"It's in here." Aiden held up his mirror. The glass showed a mass of dark, swirly stuff. Now and then two glaring eyes came to the surface. It was like looking at really angry smoke.

"If that's the boggun. . ." I broke off, looking for the shadow I'd seen slipping through the bannisters.

"There was definitely only one of them in the dungeon," Nora said anxiously. "I hope what you saw wasn't a grey phantom or a fire wraith – though I think the wraiths need to live close to volcanoes. They caused an eruption in Iceland in 1783 when the volcanic area became infested, according to the *Field Guide to Wraiths, Phantoms and Bogguns.*"

I scanned the corridor. Where had the shadow gone? Had I imagined it?

A patch of darkness lurked in a doorway. I wasn't sure it was really there until it moved. The shadow slid up the staircase and I crept after it, my blade ready. Downstairs the sound of voices grew louder as the classes came back inside.

"Robyn Silver!" Mrs Lovell called. "I hope you're not upstairs. Aiden McGee! Nora Juniper! Come down at once."

"We'll keep her talking," Aiden told me. "You get that thing. Good luck!"

I nodded. I didn't dare take my eyes off the moving shadow in case I lost it again. As it crossed a patch of light at the top of the stairs, the shadow darkened into a clearer shape – a figure with thin arms and a skirt or long coat swirling around its legs.

The shadow figure slid under the door to

Cryptorum's study and disappeared. I crept forward, but Eye scuttled past and stopped between me and the door. The little crab creature waved her claws wildly.

"What is it, Eye?" I whispered. "What's going on?"

Eye jabbed her claw at Cryptorum's study and waved her claws again.

I stepped round her, pushing the door handle quietly. "Don't worry, I'll be careful."

The study was eerily silent. The shadow figure showed no sign that it saw me as it glided over to the little white cupboard where the wish was kept. The cupboard door rattled as if shadow fingers were shaking it.

"Stop!" I held my frostblade up high. "You're not allowed in here."

The shadow whirled. It was everywhere – at the bookcase, under the desk and beside the window. At last it stopped by the fireplace and drew a silver key from just inside the chimney. I froze, watching the key float through the air. It turned slowly in the lock. It was horrible to watch.

"Robyn!" It was Cryptorum's voice.

The sound pulled me out of my terrible frozen

state. "I'm in here!" I swung my blade at the shadow but hit nothing at all. The shadow slipped to the window and edged through the tiny crack under the wooden frame.

Cryptorum dashed up the stairs and entered the study with Miss Smiting right behind him. The door to the white cupboard was swinging slightly. Inside, the wish floated around the glass case, its blue-green surface catching the light.

Cryptorum's voice was deathly quiet. "Why are you in my office without permission and WHY are you going through my things?"

"I didn't!" I stammered. "It wasn't me who opened the cupboard."

"Tell the truth, Robyn." Miss Smiting bore down on me. Her eyes were points of angry green fire. "You opened it before."

"Yes, but I didn't this time," I said desperately. "It was a shadow. It found the key up the chimney and then it slipped out of the window when it heard you coming. Honest!"

The wish inside the cupboard went crazy as Cryptorum came near, bouncing about and bashing itself against the glass. Closing the cupboard door carefully, Cryptorum turned the key and put it in his pocket.

I looked away so he wouldn't think I'd been staring, but my brain whirled. What was that wish and why didn't he want anyone to see it?

Cryptorum looked fiercer than I'd ever seen him. "Robyn Silver. You have a lot of explaining to do."

I swallowed. He was glaring so hard I thought his eyebrows might get stuck in that position.

"I trusted you," he growled. "I let you visit my study after school and now you come here and snoop around."

I tried to explain. I told them about the noises in the walls and the kobold in the ballroom. It came out in a bit of a rush – especially the part about the kobold trapped in the roasting dish. Miss Smiting hurried away when she heard this. After I'd finished, Cryptorum paced up and down a few times. Then he said, "You'd better sit down."

I slumped on to the leather sofa. I hoped I was missing something really boring downstairs – geography, maybe.

Miss Smiting reappeared. "Everything iss as she sayss – the kobold is in the kitchen and there are signs of a disturbance in the ballroom. The basement iss empty and the other Chimes gave me thiss." She held up a mirror with a smoky surface. It was the one Aiden had used to trap the boggun.

Cryptorum leant heavily on his desk. "Then we have a shadow-walker. It set the creatures from the basement free – probably to make mischief while it came up here."

I was surprised to see him look worried. "What's a shadow-walker?"

"It's a vampire – a particularly dangerous kind," he explained. "A vampire that's strong enough to walk abroad in sunlight can detach his shadow and send it to follow his commands."

I stared. "You mean their shadow goes around by itself? And it can touch things and see things?"

Cryptorum nodded. "However they can't send their shadows too far from their bodies and that means the vampire was close by."

My heart went cold. Shadows that moved by themselves. That was the creepiest thing I'd ever heard. I glanced round the room, half afraid that the vampire's shadow was still hiding somewhere.

"We musst be ready." Miss Smiting glided to Cryptorum's side. "We will help you defeat this vampire just as you beat the ones that dwelt here years ago."

Cryptorum shook his head. "That's if I can find him! One shadow-walker can easily slip along a street and into people's houses without being seen.

It will take every tracking skill I have to hunt him down."

"I can help!" I cried. "Aiden and Nora will too."

Cryptorum's face was grim. "These creatures are vicious. I can't put you in that kind of danger. A shadow-walker in town is very bad news indeed."

14

I Start to Wonder About the Hidden Wish

When I met Aiden and Nora after school, they were desperate to find out what was going on. We started climbing the stairs to the north wing but Miss Smiting caught us and swept us out to the little garden surrounded by tall hedges. We sat on a stone bench watched by a bunch of statues with spooky blank eyes.

"Mr Cryptorum is not to be disturbed," Miss Smiting told us. "He has much to think about and as sssoon as it's dark he must send out the bats."

"To look for the vampire?" I said. I was picturing someone with fangs and a big cloak.

"Yesss. Although bats can only sense a vampire once they have fed. If this one wants to remain hidden it may be difficult." Miss Smiting glided between the statues. "Mr Cryptorum left to investigate reports of vampire activity in the north two weeksss ago but by the time he found their lair, the creatures had fled."

Nora's eyes were wide. "Do you think the vampire that came here yesterday didn't feed so that the bats couldn't warn us it was coming?"

Miss Smiting nodded. "That iss exactly what I think."

"So this vampire can take off his shadow and let it walk around separately," Aiden said thoughtfully. "That must make it even harder to hunt down."

"It's definitely a neat trick." I stifled a shiver. "But how does the vampire survive without feeding?"

"Vampires can eat human food for a short time," Miss Smiting said. "They walk in both the human and the Unseen World, remember? They especially like burgers and steaksss – anything meaty, actually. But never fear – soon Erasmus will follow its tracks and vanquish the nasty creature. Just make sure you travel home together and keep your eyes open for anything suspiciousss."

"Should we look out for someone with fangs and a cloak?" I suggested, but for once neither Aiden or

Nora laughed. I guess we were all freaked out by what had happened earlier.

Miss Smiting eyed me seriously. "They could look like anyone, Robyn Silver. That is what makes them so dangerousss."

"Do you get the feeling there's something they're not telling us?" I said to Aiden on the way home.

"I reckon there's a lot they're not telling us," Aiden said. "If a vampire can get its shadow to walk right into Chime headquarters then we have a big problem. I reckon the creature already knew who Cryptorum was and what he does, and now they probably know about us too."

I shivered. "I thought Grimdean House would be safe. And the shadow went straight for that cupboard with the wish."

Aiden shrugged. "That probably doesn't mean anything. It could have been looking for something else, like weapons."

I wasn't so sure.

When I got home, I dug out the *Wishes and Mysteries* book I'd borrowed from Cryptorum's bookcase and hidden under my bed. Mum knocked on the door and I covered the book with my quilt.

"Honey, can you watch Annie and Josh for a few

minutes?" Mum said. "We've run out of milk and I've got to pop to the shop."

"Can't Ben or Sammie do it?" I jumped up, knocking a pile of stuff off my bedside table.

"Ben's gone to a friend's house and Sammie's training for this gym competition which means a lot to her. Come on – we all need to pitch in and help out."

I just managed to stop myself rolling my eyes. The "we all have to pitch in" speech was one I'd heard a billion times. I wanted to point out that it wasn't ALL of us helping out – it was just me. But I didn't because then she'd start telling me off and I'd never get back to my wish book.

"Actually – before I forget – can you bring Josh and Annie home from school tomorrow and again next Monday?" Mum went on. "I've got some delivering to do for Dazzling Design and I won't be able to get to Grimdean House for home time."

I pulled a face. Mum worked for a greeting card company, and she sorted and packed big boxes of cards which she kept in our basement. She'd never asked me to bring Annie and Josh home before though. "I can't! I'm staying for my club after school. Mr Cryptorum's expecting me to be there." I searched for a more convincing reason. "We'll be studying more creatures – nocturnal animals and stuff!"

"Robyn! You'll just have to miss Bat Club. It's only for a couple days. You spend too much time at Grimdean House anyway – you're tired and grouchy all the time. I'm a bit concerned about it to be honest." She studied me.

My stomach plunged. She wasn't about to ban me from going to Bat Club altogether, was she? I should've remembered to bring home the ice-cream-tub mouse house to remind her how lovely and educational it was. I quickly gave her a big smile. "All right! I'll fetch them home – don't worry! You go to the shop. We'll be fine here."

When she'd gone, I pulled out *Wishes and Mysteries* from under the quilt. It was just my luck to miss Chime training the week we found out there was a vampire in town. I thought of the walking shadow and stifled a shiver. It had wanted that wish. That had to mean something bad.

I flicked through the pages, reading the chapter headings. Stopping at *Wishes Made by the Very Young*, I read a bit: *Young children's wishes are the most interesting of all. The brilliant sheen—*

"Robyn!" Annie burst in, recorder in hand. "This is the new song that Miss Mason taught us today."

She began playing the tune – squeaking on all the high notes.

I hid the book again and waited for her to finish. "Awesome! All right, you'd better go. I've got homework to do."

"Don't you want me to play some more?" Annie piped a few random notes. The squeaky noise was starting to give me a headache.

"Maybe after dinner," I told her.

Annie's cheeks went pink. "You didn't like it, did you? I *wish* you'd let me play to you." She ran off, leaving a bright wish bubble floating in the air. The wish felt like silk and it didn't pop when I touched it. The bubble was clearer and brighter than any wish I'd ever made. In the centre was an image of Annie playing her recorder and me clapping and smiling. I waited for it to pop but it didn't.

I turned back to the wishes book. There had to be something in here that explained why Annie's wish looked so perfect and lasted so long. *The wishes that endure without bursting are those that are heartfelt*, I read, *while frivolous wishes that the wisher does not really mean will vanish quickly.* So that explained why Annie's wish hadn't popped. She'd really meant what she said.

I read some more. *Children's wishes appear bright,*

clear and strong because they are young and innocent. Consequently, their final wishes are the strongest of all. (See page 47) I frowned. Their final wishes. What did that mean?

Flicking forward through the book, I scanned a few paragraphs. There was a lot about final wishes. A long time ago some guy called Malcolm Malnear had watched an old lady make a wish just before she died and it had come true. She'd wished that no one should knock down her house after she was gone. Sure enough, someone had tried to do it but their axes had bounced off the wooden walls. The house was indestructible. It must have been weird to watch.

Then Malcolm Malnear had gone round the country trying to find out if other people's last wishes had come true. He found more stories proving that the same thing had happened over and over again.

I closed the book. None of this really explained why the shadow-walking vampire had been after the wish made by Mr Cryptorum's wife. Except... A horrible tingle ran down my back... Miss Smiting had told us it was her last wish before she died. I'd thought maybe Cryptorum was just being soppy. But maybe ... MAYBE he'd trapped the wish in the

189

glass case because if it got loose it could come true.

Opening the book again, I read the final sentence at the bottom of the page. *Therefore I must conclude that the last wish a person ever makes will come true, particularly when that wish is a strong one.* So why did the shadow-walking vampire want the wish? Did that mean the wish was something terrible?

"Robyn! Josh is being mean to me and he stole my recorder!" Annie yelled.

I sighed and stashed *Wishes and Mysteries* under the bed again. I needed to talk to Aiden and Nora about this.

Sammie burst in. Didn't anyone in this family ever knock? "Annie says Mum's out and you're meant to be watching her and Josh. So why are they literally destroying the living room? You're so irresponsible!"

"Why didn't *you* stop them, then?" I snapped back.

By the time I got to the living room, Josh was jumping up and down on the sofa and holding Annie's recorder out of her reach. I took it off him and wiped Annie's tears away. A shadow swept past the window, sending an icy prickle down my neck, but it was only the shadow of a tree caught in the moving headlights of a car.

A vampire in town was really bad news. A vampire that could get inside Grimdean House without being spotted was even worse. All this time I'd wanted Cryptorum and Miss Smiting to let us out to fight monsters. Now the monsters were coming to find us.

The Bird of Death Comes to Visit

iden and Nora weren't as excited by my discovery in the *Wishes and Mysteries* book as I thought they'd be.

"But people's final wishes came true," I said. "Don't you think that's amazing?"

"Are you sure they really came true?" Aiden said. "It doesn't sound very likely if you think about it."

"It was in the book!" I protested. "This guy, Malcolm, saw it happen."

"But the book's really old, right? So maybe it's just a legend." Aiden shrugged. "Anyway Cryptorum's probably only kept that wish because it was his wife's."

We were standing on the back steps of Grimdean

House after school. A weak orange sun was sinking behind the firs at the far end of the garden. My hands were freezing and my breath hung in the air like a little misty cloud. Mr Cryptorum was marching across the lawn to the weapons shed. I'd already told him why I couldn't stay late for Bat Club and he didn't seem very happy.

"I'd better go." I sighed. "Annie will get upset if I don't collect her on time. You'll have to tell me what he says about fighting vampires tomorrow."

"*The Compendium of Ancient Beasts and Fiends* says all you have to do is pierce a vampire through the heart with a silver weapon," Nora said. "I think the hard bit is spotting one because they look the same as everyone else."

Unlocking the shed, Cryptorum called across the garden. "Are you lot going to chat all day?"

"He's even grumpier than usual," Aiden said to Nora. "We'd better go."

Reluctantly, I went to find my kid brother and sister. Mrs Lovell was in her cubicle in the entrance hall chatting to Miss Mason. The music teacher swept her blonde hair over her shoulder. A large crate of tambourines stood on the floor next to her sparkly boots. I found Josh swinging off the railing in front of the mansion while Annie played earsplitting high notes on her recorder.

I took Annie's hand, which was even colder than mine. "All right, let's go."

Darkness thickened as we walked down Demus Street and the wind picked up, rocking the bare branches of the trees.

When we got in, Annie dived straight for the kitchen cupboard. Everyone in our house knew that when Mum was out, the cookies were fair game. Mum staggered through the door a few minutes later with a big sack of cards.

"You're early! Can I go back to find Aiden?" I started putting my shoes on again.

"Sure – just don't be late for tea." Mum set the sack down on the table.

A guilty feeling wriggled in my gut as I raced back to Grimdean. It was true that I'd see Aiden, but Mum probably thought I'd gone to his house. The wind had dropped and the puddles on the pavement were starting to freeze. The street lamps flickered on one after the other but I veered away from the light. Tonight it felt safer in the shadows, out of sight. I patted my pocket, checking that the torchblade was still there.

The door to Grimdean House was ajar and lights were blazing in the hallway. I was surprised the place wasn't locked up. Our secret Chime training wouldn't stay that way very long if people walked in on us. I reached the bottom of the steps just as the clock began to strike the hour. Each chime vibrated through my bones and I stared up at the golden clock face. It was strange to think this Mortal Clock had activated my special powers. It must have some pretty powerful enchantments inside.

I was thinking about that as I ran up the steps and I almost missed the tiny movement at the corner of my eye. Someone was sitting in the shadows where they could barely be seen. Blonde hair glinted under the woman's hood, and I caught a glimpse of red lipstick and pale skin. There was a plastic crate on the step below, full of tambourines.

I edged closer. "Miss Mason! Are you all right?"

The music teacher rose to her feet, pushing back her hood. Her eyes glittered in the darkness and her red-and-silver scarf was wound tightly round her throat. "Robyn, what are you doing here? Did you forget something?" She gave me a shiny smile.

I hesitated. Why was she talking so loudly and slowly? Did she think I couldn't hear very well? "No, I just came to see Aiden. He stayed late today."

"Well, I'm just waiting for a lift." She indicated

the crate of tambourines. "I don't want to carry these all the way home, do I?"

Honestly, she was acting as if she was talking to a five-year-old. "Bye, Miss Mason." I went inside but the teacher put her hand on the door before I could close it.

She followed me into the brightly lit entrance hall. "Maybe I should come with you. I'm sure you don't want to wander round such a big old house by yourself!"

"It's OK! I know where to find him." The last thing I wanted was for Miss Mason to discover Cryptorum training the others. I needed to get away and warn them that she was still here.

Miss Mason lowered her voice, her eyes full of concern. "Nothing's wrong is it? You seem a bit anxious."

Something *was* wrong. Why was she hanging around like this? I dropped my gaze, suddenly afraid I was giving my thoughts away. The fake diamonds on her boots glittered in the light. Something stirred in my memory. *Her boots were studded with rhinestones.*

"You wait here," she suggested. "I'll go and look for your friend."

"I can find him. Don't worry." I frowned. I knew

something about boots decorated with rhinestones. There was something weird going on here. What was it?

I studied her very closely and suddenly I realized exactly what was wrong with her.

Miss Mason had no shadow.

Mine was stretched behind me across the floor and joined to me at my feet. The bright electric light here in the hallway made my shadow dark with clear-cut edges. I shifted and it moved with me. But there was nothing joined to Miss Mason.

A horrible cold feeling slithered all the way down my throat. If Miss Mason had no shadow that meant she'd sent it somewhere else. It was shadow-walking right now – probably round this house – all by itself. If Miss Mason could shadow-walk then she had to be a vampire.

I was standing right beside one of the most dangerous creatures of the Unseen World.

But she might not know that I was on to her. My pulse raced. I forced myself to look at her and smile. My hand rested on the torchblade in my pocket. What had Nora said? Pierce her heart with silver? But she looked like a *person*. She was the music teacher!

I chickened out. "Sorry, I've got to go."

"Not yet!" She grabbed my arm with fingers like cold steel.

I tried to push her off. Her smile vanished and her eyes burned like black fire. Dark veins bulged from her pale cheeks. Gripping on to me, she raised her other arm. I pulled out my torchblade and flicked the sword open. The silver blade gleamed and she released me in surprise.

Dodging round her, I ran off down the passageway. I had to find Cryptorum and the others. It was pitch-black and my steps echoed in the silence. I stopped and listened for footsteps following me, but the only thing I could hear was my heart hammering in panic. Was there movement in the darkness? I could see so little – I might not know until it was too late. Goosebumps rose on my arms. Holding my sword ready, I switched on the light.

The corridor was empty.

I shuddered, remembering the black veins spread across the vampire's face. Why hadn't I realized what Miss Mason was? I was a Chime – I should've known. Why had she come here in disguise? She'd been here for weeks – teaching classes and running a recorder group. Annie was in that group too. My stomach lurched. Something terrible could have happened and I wouldn't have been able to stop it.

Running to the back door, I found it was locked and there was no key. On the stone paving in front of the lawn was a massive bird, bigger than a large dog, with black feathers and a beak as sharp as a blade. It was like no bird I'd ever seen and it had a nasty watchful look, as if it was wondering whether I tasted nice.

I rattled the door again but there was no way to open it and I couldn't see Cryptorum or the others. Did they know about the monster bird? Maybe they'd come inside to get away from it. Swinging round, I made for the stairs, taking them in twos. By the time I got to the north wing, my lungs were ready to explode.

As soon as I stopped, I heard music. A soft melody was drifting from Cryptorum's study and light gleamed under the door. I huffed. There was a gigantic black-feathered bird in the garden and I'd nearly been kidnapped by a vampire, and here were my friends having a nice relaxing time.

I opened the door. "Guys!" I stopped.

Miss Smiting was kneeling on the carpet, her body swaying slightly, while a long reedy pipe floated above her in mid-air. The snake-woman's expression was blank and her arms hung limply by her side. There was nobody playing the pipe but I knew the snake charmer had to be Miss Mason.

Across the room, a shadow darted beside the bookcase. Books zoomed off the shelves – their pages turning in one long flick from beginning to end – then each one thumped on to the floor, adding to a growing pile.

I'd found Miss Mason's shadow.

I froze, uncertain whether to hide or draw my sword. The shadow showed no sign of having noticed me. The books kept flying off the shelves and landing on the floor. I glanced quickly at the white cupboard where Mrs Cryptorum's last wish was kept. It had been shut tight with two large padlocks.

Creeping round the desk, I knelt down beside Miss Smiting. Her slit-like pupils had narrowed to thin black lines and she looked as if she was locked in a dream.

"Miss Smiting, are you all right?" I whispered.

Her gaze was fixed on the pipe and she never glanced at me. The music made me think of dry dusty lands and strange fruit. I took the snake-woman's arm and shook her. "Miss Smiting! Wake up!"

Her eyelids flickered. She was in there somewhere. I was sure of it.

Half the bookshelves were empty now. Maybe if I grabbed the instrument I could stop the music and bring Miss Smiting out of her trance. I watched the pipe, ready to make a move. . .

Something stirred right above me. A thick book hovered overhead. Brown cover, gold lettering – *smack!*

Pain blasted through my skull and everything suddenly went black.

When I opened my eyes, Nora was leaning over me and something wet was dripping down my forehead.

"Urgh!" I pulled off the wet tissue. "What's that for?"

"I thought it might make you feel better." Nora helped me sit up. The room whirled a bit and I tried to focus. Why was everyone looking at me? Cryptorum was shooting me ferocious glances in between striding up and down the room, which he was finding tricky because of the mass of books on the floor.

I remembered – the shadow, the pipe, Miss Mason.

"Miss Mason's the vampire!" I blurted out.

"No, she isn't!" Aiden stared. "She teaches recorders. Don't worry, Robyn, everything's going to be fine. You've just bumped your head that's all."

I tried to stand up but the room started whirling again. "It's true! She *is* the vampire. I saw her outside and she was acting really weird, and she had no shadow. Then I came up here and the shadow was pulling books off the shelves."

"Who is this Mason?" Cryptorum demanded. "Why are you even up here, Robyn? You tell me you can't come to training and then I find all this!" He gestured to the piles of books.

"Miss Mason's our music teacher." I told him what I'd seen, adding every little thing I could remember. His expression changed as I described the black veins criss-crossing Miss Mason's cheeks. "Then I found the shadow in here and it was like Miss Smiting had been hypnotized."

Miss Smiting was sitting on the sofa with her head in her hands. She looked up with a faint hiss. "I wass snake-charmed, my dear. That monster! She knew what my weakness would be. I remember the music ssstarting to play and then nothing."

"But what do you think she was doing?" Nora said. "Why go for the books?"

"It isn't clear what this creature is up to!" Cryptorum started pacing again. "But the bats have sensed nothing so she can't be feeding. My guess is that this is the same vampire that sent their shadow in before. I'd never have thought she'd have the nerve to return!"

I tried to think but my head was pounding. "There was something that made me remember that vampire you told us about, Miss Smiting. It was the fake diamonds on her boots."

Miss Smiting rose to her feet. "You are talking of Pearl! It cannot be! I would have recognized her. I have ssseen this Miss Mason in the corridor with her recorders and tambouriness. She does not look like Pearl."

"But the black veins. . . I've read something about that," Nora began.

"The black veins are a sign of dark enchantment." Cryptorum looked grim. "She may have changed her whole appearance – face-shifted. If I'd seen her I might have recognized some of the other signs, but I never did."

I suddenly remembered Miss Mason rushing out when Cryptorum was heard coming along the corridor. I'd thought she was just nervous about meeting him because he sounded so fierce.

"Could it really be her?" Miss Smiting said.

"It sounds like her," Cryptorum growled. "The last time we met I fought her along the back alleys of Wendleton. She was wounded but she was still very strong. I tried to finish her off right then but she managed to escape. She promised me she'd be back one day for revenge."

"But that was so many years ago." The snake-woman frowned.

"Time means nothing to a vampire. I should've defeated her once and for all back then." Cryptorum's hand went to the blade under his coat. "Go home, all of you. Pearl is a powerful enemy and if this shadow-walker is her then no one is safe. There will be no more Bat Club until I've found and killed her." He swung the door open and we heard his heavy tread on the stairs.

"Wasn't Pearl the leader of the vampires before Mr Cryptorum drove them out of town?" I said.

"Indeed she was. We do not know for certain if this vampire is Pearl but if it is..." Miss Smiting twisted her hands. "I think you should know that Pearl was the one that killed Erasmus's wife, Rebecca Cryptorum. It happened a long time ago. The vampire caught them unawaress one day. Erasmus fought her and in the confusion Rebecca was knocked down. She never fully recovered from the blow and died seven days later."

"No wonder he hates that vampire so much!" I said.

"Erasmus wass wild with grief. He fought monsters night after night without resting. He broke the Mortal Clock and swore he'd never let anyone else in Wendleton be cursed with Chime powers." Miss Smiting glided to the door. "Go home, children, and do not venture out again till morning. I shall ssee this place is locked up." She hurried out of the room.

"Poor Mr Cryptorum! It's sad and romantic at the same time," Nora said. "To lose the person you love like that..."

"Made him as grouchy as he is today," I finished. I did feel sorry for Cryptorum though. It was obvious his life hadn't been easy. I wobbled a little as I stood up.

"Are you all right now, Robyn?" Nora offered me the wet tissue again.

"I'm OK!" I picked up a thick book with gold lettering lying by my feet. It had to be the book the shadow had hit me with. The title read *How to Relax and Find Inner Peace*. "Great!" I muttered. "Trust me to be knocked out by that."

"Don't faint again," Aiden told me. "We've got to get home."

"It was horrible seeing you lying still like that," Nora gabbled as we went downstairs. "And all the books thrown everywhere."

"Where were you guys anyway?" I asked. "I couldn't see you in the garden."

"We went into town," Aiden said. "Cryptorum saw the bats leave the barn in a rush and we followed them. We took weapons and everything!"

"What? Not fair!" I cried. "I didn't know there'd be a trip out. What was the monster?"

"A grodder! Strange to see one right in the middle of town. I hit it with an arrow before Mr Cryptorum destroyed it," Nora said proudly.

"Huh! And I thought you'd just run away from that evil-looking bird. What was that thing anyway?" My friends' faces told me they didn't know what I was talking about. "I saw it outside. It had black feathers and a really sharp beak. It was massive – bigger than a dog."

We'd reached the entrance hall where Miss Smiting was checking the locks on the windows.

"Hold on a minute! You saw a huge black bird with a sharp beak?" Nora screwed up her face as if she was trying to remember something. "*With beak that pierces bone and feathers black as coal, the etting hunts you down to take your mortal soul."*

"Geez!" I didn't like the sound of that. It might have been the beak that pierces bone part. "What did you call it?"

"An etting. Legends say that they can predict who will die. Once they've found someone who won't live long, they follow them around to feed on their departing soul as they take their final breath."

I swallowed. I suddenly realized I was the only one to have seen the bird. Somehow I didn't feel too great about that.

We Use a Ton of Garlic

I slept badly. My dreams were full of birds with knife-like beaks and music teachers with gigantic fangs. The birds opened their beaks and began a strange screeching song. I woke with a start. Annie was sitting on her bed, playing her recorder.

"Annie, cut it out!" I cried. "It's six-thirty!"

Annie's face crumpled and tears came to her eyes. Feeling bad, I went over and put an arm round her. "Sorry! You just woke me from this weird dream that's all. Why don't you play after breakfast?"

"But I'm getting really good." She clutched the instrument tight. "I'm one of the best in our recorder group and I can play most of 'Jingle Bells'."

"That's great." I gave her a squeeze. I didn't tell

her that recorder group was probably over now. She wouldn't see Miss Mason again. Not if Cryptorum got hold of her first.

I left early, grabbing a piece of toast to eat on the way. I wanted to find out if Cryptorum had traced the vampire and whether he had a plan. I dashed down the street, almost slipping on the icy pavement. Frost edged the tree branches like a furry white caterpillar.

As I turned into Demus Street, I saw the limo parked up in front of the mansion. Cryptorum was loading duffle bags into the boot. I could guess what was in them – weapons. There was a large wooden chest stowed inside too.

"Last one!" Aiden emerged from the house carrying another bag. Miss Smiting followed with a map tucked under her arm.

Nora ran up behind me. "Are they leaving?"

"Looks like it," I said.

Cryptorum waited as we gathered round. "Pearl – that's the vampire you know as Miss Mason – has fled town. I caught sight of her on the westbound road last night but she was too fast for me." He grimaced. "Mr Dray's found where she may have been hiding. There's an abandoned farmhouse to the north of Kesterly Manor where lights have been seen at night. It could be that Pearl is forming a vampire gang and planning an attack."

"Mr Dray and those kids will find her, won't they?" Nora said eagerly. "They've got those special scanners."

"Flashy gadgets are no substitute for the instincts of a Chime!" Cryptorum snapped. "Half the time those scanners just pick up fox trails. In any case, Mr Dray doesn't agree that Pearl could be gathering other vampires. He's decided that one vampire isn't a good use for his precious resources so I doubt they'll help any further."

"You mean they can't be bothered?" I said. "But Miss Mason got inside this house!"

"Quiet, Robyn! We're don't want everyone hearing." Cryptorum glanced round.

"Dray has alwayss put money first," Miss Smiting hissed. "He never doess anything for nothing."

Cryptorum scowled and handed me a key. "Here's the key to the shed. Find the big bag of garlic on the bottom shelf and crush some on every window sill and door frame in the house. If any more vampires come into town it will keep them at bay."

"Does that really work?" I said. "It's just a vegetable, isn't it?"

"It works," Cryptorum said shortly. "Wendleton is yours to defend. Remember – some vampires can walk in sunlight. Try not to do anything stupid – and remember to feed the bats, please. Their food's in the shed too." He climbed into the limo and Miss Smiting got into the driving seat.

Aiden exchanged looks with me as the limo roared up the street. "Looks like we're in charge then."

"I can't believe that Mr Dray won't help Cryptorum." I folded my arms to keep out the cold. "Especially when he has all that equipment."

"Maybe he'll change his mind and they'll track down Pearl together," Nora said.

Aiden held the front door open. "We haven't got much time. We'd better get on with finding the garlic."

We raced down to the shed, dug out the garlic and squashed it on to the window sills and door frames. Even though we spread the stuff out, we only completed the downstairs rooms before it was gone.

"We can buy some more after school," I whispered to Aiden in French class.

"Ugh, Robyn! You stink!" Hector hissed as he dumped a *Textbook Français* on my desk.

I sniffed my hand when no one was looking and my head swam. I'd forgotten to wash my hands after crushing the garlic. It wasn't just vampires that this stuff repelled.

The wind whistled round the house all day, and yellow-grey clouds hurried across the sky, heavy with snow that didn't fall. After school ended we went to Lipson's groceries, but all we managed to find was powdered garlic in a jar.

"Do you think it'll work the same?" Nora asked doubtfully as Aiden and me shook the powder over the window sills upstairs.

"It'll have to do." Aiden took the jar and headed into Cryptorum's study.

I hung back, my stomach turning over. I couldn't help remembering last night and the shadow pulling the books off the shelves. I thought of Miss Smiting hypnotized by the pipe music – what other horrible skills did Miss Mason have?

Nora noticed my expression. "What is it, Robyn?"

I didn't want to admit to being scared, especially to Nora who was a year younger than me and Aiden. I made myself walk into the room which was now completely tidy with every book back on the shelf. The padlocks were still on the wish cupboard. "I was thinking about Miss Mason and why she pretended to be working here for weeks."

"She must have wanted to know what Cryptorum was up to so she used the shadow-walking to look around." Aiden shook the last of the garlic powder over the window sill.

"That's the last room, isn't it? No vampire can get in now," Nora said with forced cheerfulness. "Let's go and feed the bats before we go home."

As we ran down the garden, a handful of snowflakes drifted from the sky. Darkness was falling and the wind was a blast of ice against my face. I took out the key Cryptorum had given me and unlocked the shed. On a shelf inside were three trays of overripe peaches and mangoes which we'd spotted that morning while hunting for the garlic. But something else caught my eye.

I took the special frostblade from the weapons rack and pulled it from its sheath. The silver blade gleamed and its swirly markings looked like an alphabet from ancient times. I swung it back and forth just to test it out. It felt so much stronger than the practice swords and torchblades I'd used. I was desperate to borrow it and try it out properly but I was sure Cryptorum would know.

I reluctantly put it away. "So what do we do – just leave the fruit outside for them?" I asked Nora.

She shrugged. "I dunno. I've never read anything about looking after bats."

This was a bit of a shock. I had begun to think

Nora knew everything. I leant down to get a tray just as a dark figure appeared in the doorway making me spill fruit across the floor.

"You young'uns are here late." Obediah Brown's gnarled face came into view. He wore an old grey overcoat and his hands were covered in mud. "You have to leave the bat food inside the barn. That's what Cryptorum does."

"Thanks – we'll do that," I said, scooping up the peaches.

"And be careful." He disappeared into the dusk. "There's danger about tonight. I can feel it in my bones."

The flurry of snow petered out, leaving a dusting of white across the grass. We carried the fruit to the bat barn and the smell inside made my head spin. Rows of little dark creatures hung from the rafters. I got the feeling they'd been waiting for us. We set down the fruit and backed away as, one by one, the bats spread their leathery wings and dropped to the floor. Crawling over the fruit, their black eyes shone in the darkness.

"I still don't like them that much," I said.

"I think they're kinda cool," Aiden said. "And useful too. Cryptorum's taken some with him to help track the vampire."

"They haven't helped much with that so far."
I dropped my voice. I knew the bats couldn't
understand me – but still. "Otherwise we'd have
spotted what Miss Mason really was sooner."

"They can only detect a vampire when they feed,"
Nora reminded me. "She must have been getting by
on human food."

We backed out of the door, leaving the fruit to
the crawling, flapping bats. Night had fallen now
and I couldn't even see to the end of the garden.
Grimdean House was protected with garlic but
out here anything could reach us. Suddenly I was
desperate to leave but I didn't know how to say it
without sounding chicken.

"I wonder what Miss Mason really wanted, last
night," Nora said suddenly. "Her shadow had taken
every single book off the shelves as if she hadn't
really found what she was looking for."

"Weird . . . when I saw her shadow the first time
it went straight to the cupboard with the wish." I
broke off.

"What is it?" Aiden asked me.

"The shadow was searching for a book, and we
all chose books and took them home days ago. What
if the book she wanted *wasn't there* – because one of
us has it?" I said.

"Well I've got *Spring Mechanisms in Bows and Catapults*," Aiden said. "Why would she want that?"

"I've got *Unseen Creatures of the Lake and Swamp*," Nora frowned. "And you took *Advanced Moves With a Frostblade*, didn't you?"

"I took another one called *Wishes and Mysteries*." I ducked as a bat brushed my head with its wing. "Miss Mason must know I have Chime powers. Her shadow was there when I trapped the kobold in the kitchen and she saw me here again last night. What if she tries to look for the book at my house?"

"Oh, Robyn, that's horrible!" Nora gasped.

"But Cryptorum's tracking her now," Aiden reminded me. "He caught sight of her leaving town and Mr Dray had clues to where she might have been hiding."

"What if they're both wrong? What if she's still here?" A nasty fluttery feeling was growing inside my chest as if a bat was trapped inside me.

"I'm sure everything's fine," Aiden said. "Let's get some more garlic and you can put it all round your house just to be sure."

We ran back to Lipson's. Rows of newly hung Christmas lights flashed outside the toyshop and the hairdressers. The shop assistant looked at us like we were crazy when we bought three more jars of powdered garlic.

Sticking one of the garlic jars in my pocket, I rushed out of the shop with Nora and Aiden behind me. I sped round a corner, sliding on the snowy pavement. The Christmas lights on the houses were flashing on and off like a disco. I glanced up at a model sleigh fixed to a rooftop and caught sight of a black shape skimming over the trees. I couldn't see it properly in the dark, but a picture of an etting – the bird that followed those who were to die soon – flashed through my mind.

I heard Aiden shout behind me. I waved and ran on. He and Nora would be going back to put garlic around their own homes.

I turned into our street, past more houses strung with Christmas lights, and ran along our alley. A Christmas tree was propped against the back wall, ready to go inside and have every piece of tinsel we owned flung on its branches by Josh and Annie. Gasping for breath, I burst through the back door.

Mum shrieked, dropping a mixing bowl and spilling flour all over the floor.

"What is it? What's happened?" I panted.

"You did!" Mum picked up the bowl and dumped it in the sink. "I thought you were a burglar."

"Sorry! I've just got to—" I ran upstairs without finishing the sentence. Annie wasn't in our bedroom, so I dived straight under the bed for the books. My heart skipped a beat when I found them. The frostblade book and *Wishes and Mysteries*. They were both there! The tight knot that had grown inside my stomach relaxed. Everything was OK. Miss Mason hadn't been here and neither had her shadow – she probably didn't know where I lived anyway. Now I would spread the garlic round the doors and windows – just to be sure.

I rushed round the house with the jar of garlic, sprinkling powder on the window sills. Josh was in the bathroom, so I did his room quickly. Sammie screeched when I opened her door and threw her lipstick at me. I thought of not bothering with her room, but then I tossed some garlic on to her window sill before she shoved me out of the door.

"Robyn?" Mum called up the stairs. "What's going on up there?"

"Nothing!" I stashed the garlic in my pocket. I just had the front door and downstairs windows left to do. Ben was in the front room watching a football match on TV so I had to creep in and sprinkle the garlic when he was shouting at the referee and totally oblivious to anything else.

I dashed back to the kitchen. "Sorry! What's for tea?"

"It's pizza." Mum took the tinfoil off a plate and set it in front of me. There were six slices on it – not bad. "It's the only thing I can get all four of you to eat." Mum added.

"Annie doesn't eat it." I bit into the first slice. "She hates cheese."

Mum turned back to the washing-up. "Is she a friend from school?"

"No, I'm talking about our Annie," I said.

Mum scrubbed a saucepan and let the foamy water drip off before setting it on the draining board. "I don't know who you mean."

"My little sister," I said impatiently. Glancing at the coat pegs in the hallway, I saw that Annie's red coat wasn't there. Her shoes with the purple butterflies weren't by the back door either. "Where is Annie anyway?"

Mum turned to face me and wiped her hands on her apron. "What are you talking about, Robyn? Who's Annie?"

I Make a Wish
for My Sister

here was a buzzing in my ears. Why was she being like this? "You know who I mean – Annie! Little kid, always playing her recorder. My *sister*!"

Mum looked confused. "Is this some new name you're calling Sammie? I wish you two would try and get along a bit better. You're lucky to have a sister. I just had brothers when I was growing up. And Sammie's doing so well at school – she could help you with your homework."

"I'm not talking about Sammie. I'm talking about Annie." I put down the pizza. "Mum, please! You know – our Annie!"

"Look – I don't know the names of all your friends." Mum frowned. "I don't know any children round here called Annie."

The bottom dropped out of my world. The kitchen clock ticked on the wall. The fridge made the whistling-gurgling noise it always did, but nothing was the same.

"Annie's my sister!" I whispered. "She's the youngest – the little one."

Mum was looking at me like I was mad. "Do you feel feverish?" She put a hand on my forehead. "You don't feel very hot."

I wheeled round and ran up the stairs to the bedroom I shared with my sister. Everything was still there – her furry toys and her unicorn book. Her white dressing gown with the pink heart pattern was hanging over a chair, and her school bag and recorder lay on the floor beside her bed.

Mum had followed me. "What's the matter, Robyn? Is this Annie another girl from your class? Have you fallen out with her?"

I swallowed a huge lump in my throat. "No! Annie's your daughter! Look at this stuff – it's all hers! We sleep here together."

Mum clutched her hair. "You're not making any sense! This is your room. It's been your room for years. The extra bed is a spare one."

"Don't you remember how she plays the recorder all the time? How she never eats vegetables? How she wakes up stupidly early in the mornings?" I picked up Annie's dressing gown and shook it. "Look – this isn't mine! It's way too small."

"OK, it's all right," Mum said soothingly. "Just . . . relax. You're obviously not very well. I'm going to get you some medicine and then I'll make you a honey and lemon drink." She pulled back Annie's quilt. "Hop into bed and I'll be back in a minute." She hurried back downstairs and I heard her turn the kettle on.

I sank on to Annie's bed, holding her dressing gown tightly.

Something terrible must have happened to make Mum forget Annie. You didn't just forget that one of your kids existed – not without something serious being done to you.

My head spun. Where *was* Annie? It was past six o'clock. Even if she'd gone to a friend's place to play she'd be back by now. I ran into Sammie's room and pulled off her headphones. "Where's Annie? Is she at a friend's house?"

"Get off me, you freak!" Sammie snapped. "What are you doing?"

"I just want to know where Annie is."

"I don't know who you're talking about. Get out of my room!" She put her headphones back on.

My heart plunged and I raced into Josh's room. "Hey, Josh. Where's Annie?"

He didn't look up – too busy digging a pencil into the carpet. "Who?"

"Annie – your sister." I crouched beside him.

"You're my sister."

"I know – but Annie is too. You remember her, don't you?"

Josh gazed at me blankly and my stomach twisted.

There were voices in the kitchen followed by footsteps on the stairs. Returning to my room, I sat on Annie's bed and stared at her toys. The last thing I wanted was for Mum to come back and give me medicine and make me lie here in Annie's bed. I couldn't stand it. There was a strand of Annie's golden hair on the pillow. How could they have forgotten her?

I picked up her favourite teddy, Mr Huggle, and touched his dark brown fur. Someone or something had *made* my family forget about Annie. Whatever that was must have taken her away too. It had to be some kind of monster. Did Miss Mason have the power to do this? She'd snake-charmed Miss

Smiting with her music so maybe she could, but why would she want Annie?

"Robyn, are you OK?" Ben stood in the doorway.

"I'm fine," I said, even though my head was pounding. "Ben, can I ask you something?"

"Course." He gave his normal wide grin.

"Whose teddy is this?"

"It's yours. This is your room, remember? Mum's right, you need to lie down for a bit."

The thumping in my head grew fiercer. "Please, Ben. Say you remember Annie. Please."

Ben's forehead creased. "I know an Annie at school but she's in my maths class and you've never met her."

Mum came in carrying a tray. "Here we are. Have some medicine and then I've got some lovely hot honey and lemon for you and some of the gingerbread your teacher left." She set the tray down on the bedside table. On it was a brown medicine bottle and spoon, a steaming mug and a plate with some gingerbread on it.

I didn't want medicine. I wanted to think. "Mum, I really am fine." I got up, still holding Mr Huggle. Annie would have been excited to go with Miss Mason. She loved the recorder group. She'd never have thought she was in danger.

"Hmm, well." Mum shook the medicine bottle. "I'd like you to take this anyway. You're quite pale. I hope they're not overworking you at school. You've been spending too much time at that Bat Club – staying late all the time – and now you've caught a fever."

"I'm not ill!" The room swam a bit as I said this and Mum muttered something to Ben. I sank on to the bed again. The hot drink looked nice and so did the gingerbread. Mum poured a spoonful of medicine from the bottle. "Here you are."

I had to swallow it. The bitter taste stuck to my tongue. Maybe something sweet would take the horrible flavour away. I picked up the gingerbread. It smelt delicious. It was quite a big piece in the shape of a house with a door and windows outlined in chocolaty-brown icing.

The gingerbread your teacher left.

"Who did you say brought this?" My mouth was watering.

Mum fastened the lid back on the medicine bottle. "What's that?"

"You said someone brought the gingerbread round."

"Oh, it was a teacher, but I can't remember her name," Mum said with a vague look on her face.

"But what did she look like?" The smell of gingerbread filled my nostrils.

"She was a very friendly lady with long blonde hair and a red-and-silver scarf."

I dropped the gingerbread as if it was infected. "It was Miss Mason, wasn't it?"

"Is that the nice music teacher? I've seen her going into Grimdean House with her instruments. Yes, she brought us a whole tin of gingerbread. She's giving them out to all the pupils who've worked hard this term, she said. Isn't that nice? It's really delicious – we've all had some. The only trouble is once you've eaten a piece you just want more and more. This is the very last bit."

I stared in horror. Miss Mason had poisoned them. Was this all because of me? She knew I was a Chime – someone born to hunt her down – so she'd decided to take revenge on my family before I could even start.

"Can you remember anything else?" I said desperately. "Did you see which way she went? Because I'd love to ... knock on her door and say thank you tomorrow."

"Not really. She said something about a party though." Mum wrinkled her forehead. "I remember her talking about a special place – a House of

Sweets – yes that was it!" She gave a little laugh. "Sounds like an interesting place for a party. Have a rest now, Robyn, and I'll check on you in a little while." She smiled and picked up the tray, leaving the gingerbread behind.

After they'd gone, I sneaked down to the phone in the hallway and called Aiden. "Something terrible's happened." I told him about my family and the gingerbread. "And now Annie's gone."

"She's not the only one." Aiden's voice crackled on the other end of the line. "Finlay from next door's vanished too. My mum was asking his parents where he was and it was like they didn't even remember him."

"Is that the boy with dark hair who always waves at you? He's in the same class as Annie."

"Yeah, that's him." Aiden paused. "Stay there. I'll fetch Nora and come over."

I stood by my bedroom window. I didn't want to wait here for Aiden and Nora. I wanted to do something. Miss Mason had bewitched my family and taken Annie away.

Silently, I wished with all my strength that my little sister was sitting here with me. The wish bubble slipped from my mouth and drifted sadly to the ceiling. It had a bright picture of Annie inside it – all blue eyes and gappy teeth, her hair curling on her shoulders. It was the clearest, brightest wish I'd ever done but it still wasn't as bright as the ones Annie made.

Something prickled inside my mind.

I pulled out *Wishes and Mysteries* and scanned the bit about young children's wishes and how strong they are. Then I flicked forwards, looking for the section on last wishes. I'd read all about it after discovering Mrs Cryptorum's final wish in that glass case. Turning another page, I stopped suddenly. Shock pulsed through me as if I'd touched a red-hot pan.

The page about last wishes had been removed. It had been done carefully but you could see the tiny edge of torn paper at the centre. I remembered most of the chapter quite well. It had described how final wishes could come true. Then, with fingers like ice, I turned back to the sentence I'd just reread on the earlier page: *Children's wishes appear bright, clear and strong because they are young and innocent. Consequently, their final wishes are the strongest of all.*

I felt sick.

Miss Mason had been here, in my home. She could've used shadow-walking to search through my stuff while talking to my mum and giving out gingerbread. I'd been right – she was trying to find out more about wishes. Now she had all the information she needed.

I couldn't stop staring at the sentence: *Their last wishes are the strongest of all.*

"Robyn!"

I jumped, nearly dropping the book.

Aiden came in with Nora. "Are you all right? Your mum said we can't stay long. She says you're ill."

"I'm not ill." I thrust the book at them. "Miss Mason's been here, and see which page she ripped out – the one about final wishes and how they can come true. Now she's taken Annie and Finlay away and maybe other little kids too."

Aiden frowned. "You think she's taken the little kids for their wishes. But why?"

I swallowed. I felt like there was a lump of ice in my throat. "If she can get a wish to come true she can have anything she wants – ANYTHING! And little kids can make the strongest last wishes of all. It says so in here!"

Nora went white. "You mean she's going to make them say a final wish. . ." She tailed off.

None of us wanted to say it. There was only one way to turn someone's wish into their very last one and that was to kill them. If I didn't find Annie tonight I might never see her again.

Outside the window, a large winged shape flew over the roofs of the houses, silhouetted against the darkening sky. I threw the book down and drew my torchblade. My hands were shaking. "I'm going vampire hunting."

Aiden drew his sword too. His face was grim.

"We're coming with you," said Nora.

We Search for the House of Sweets

 left a note for Mum on my pillow saying I'd gone out with Aiden and she shouldn't worry. Hopefully she wouldn't even notice I was gone. We closed the front door quietly and raced to the end of the street.

"Wait!" Nora said breathlessly. "Do you know where you're going, Robyn?"

"Miss Mason bewitched my family with gingerbread." I took out the gingerbread house which I'd stuffed into my pocket before we left. "My mum told me she spoke of a party in a *House of Sweets* and that must be where she's taking Annie, but I don't know where it is."

"We need to find out if anyone's seen her go by,"

Aiden said. "With that blonde hair and silver scarf she's pretty easy to spot."

"I have another idea." Nora's eyes lit up. "Remember that night Miss Mason's shadow raided the books in Cryptorum's study? You were at Grimdean House, Robyn, and we were fighting that grodder in the middle of town. Well I reckon that was a distraction – Miss Mason set the grodder loose to lure us out of Grimdean and out of her way. Grodders are stupid monsters and easily controlled. You wouldn't normally find them in a town either."

"So she brought the grodder here on purpose," I said. "How does that help?"

"Just think! Where else have we seen a grodder?" Nora said.

"You mean on Blagdurn Heath the night that grodder charged us?" I pictured the grodder beast with its red eyes. "It was standing right by a ruined house – weird because I'd never seen a house up there before."

"Exactly!" Nora nodded.

"Then that could be her lair," Aiden said. "It makes sense that she'd want to be somewhere away from people. There's less chance of her being caught."

"And it's just like that story with the two lost

children, you know?" Nora added. "And the House of Sweets is like—"

"The Gingerbread House from *Hansel and Gretel*! And that makes her the witch." I threw the gingerbread on the ground and crushed it with the heel of my trainer. I tried not to think of Annie trapped inside Miss Mason's lair. I just had to focus on finding the place and then I'd get her out.

"We should go back to Grimdean and get more weapons," Aiden said. "All I have is my torchblade and that might not be enough. She's not just any vampire – remember how she can walk in sunlight."

I knew what he was trying to say. Miss Mason was obviously really powerful. She'd already tricked Cryptorum twice – first she'd tricked her way into Grimdean House and then she'd made sure he saw her leaving town. She must have laid a trail to get him out of Wendleton before doubling back. "We haven't got time. They could've left ages ago."

Aiden stood firm. "We need bows and arrows, and more garlic."

"All right! But we have to get it fast." Sprinting down the street, I dodged round the parked cars and headed for Grimdean. Now I'd thought about it, there was a weapon there I needed too.

*

Our breath hung in the icy air as we stood beside the high wall surrounding Grimdean garden.

"We'll have to shin up there," I told Aiden. "I've got a key to the shed but there's no way we'll get into the house and Obediah will have left hours ago."

"Gimme your foot then." Aiden gave me a boost and I scrambled to the top of the wall before pulling him up beside me. The wall was seven feet high and I jarred my ankle on the way down but my heart was beating so fast I hardly felt it. Unlocking the shed door with cold, stiff fingers, we helped ourselves to stuff – a bow each, quivers of arrows and torch batteries. Nora had gone to buy more garlic – if there was any left in the shop – so we got things for her too.

"Silver through the heart kills a vampire," I muttered to myself, taking Cryptorum's best frostblade from the rack. I walked out of the shed just as the moon appeared from behind a cloud, casting pale light across the garden and showing up the swirly markings along the silver blade.

"Cryptorum will be really mad at you for taking his sword," Aiden told me.

I swished the blade in a smooth arc above my head. It was a little wider than my torchblade but it felt so right in my hand. "Cryptorum's not here.

Anyway I reckon he'll forgive me if I use it to beat a vampire."

We slung the bows and arrows on our shoulders and climbed back over the wall. Nora was waiting for us on the corner. "They'd run out of garlic powder," she told us. "So I had to get garlic butter and a garlic baguette instead." She showed us her shopping bag.

"Oh, man!" I bit my lip. "Well, there's no time to get anything else."

We ran through the streets, dodging into a side road every time we saw other people. There was no way to hide the bows and arrows and we didn't want a load of questions.

At last we reached the edge of town and the ground sloped upwards towards the heath. It was dark out here with no street lights. We followed the main road up the hill, diving into the ditch every time we saw car headlights. We stopped at the top to catch our breath. Wendleton lay below us – a carpet of little orange lights and tiny rooftops. Snow started to fall again, drifting down as gently as a dream.

I pulled up my hood. It was even colder up here and every muscle in my legs hurt from the steep climb. I hoped Nora's guess about the grodder and the location of Miss Mason's lair was right. Blagdurn Heath was the last place in the world I'd have wanted to come to and it looked even more of a wasteland than it had a month ago. The bushes had lost their leaves and were little more than clumps of thin branches sticking out of the earth. The muddy ground had frozen into deep ruts and now snow was dusting over the ice. Was Annie up here? Was the vampire already making them say wishes? I had to find this House of Sweets fast.

We struck out across the heath, passing the place with the large boulder where Cryptorum had waited for us the time before. Every direction looked pretty much the same – bushes, ditches, bare branches all flecked with white.

"Which way was the ruined house?" I said.

"Over here." Aiden led us down a muddy track.

A rustling began in the undergrowth and a spiny face peered out from a patch of brambles. Drawing my frostblade, I pointed the sword at the bush and the face withdrew. That kobold did the right thing. I was in no mood to mess around.

The trees became thicker the further we went. I was starting to wonder if we'd gone the wrong way.

"Get your weapons ready." Aiden notched an arrow into his bow. "Miss Mason's probably rigged up all kinds of defences. We don't want her to know we're coming till the very last minute."

We crept on, wincing every time a twig snapped, and at last I caught the scent of something sweet. "Can you smell that?" I whispered. "It's like candy floss." I sniffed the air, trying to work out which way it was coming from.

"It reminds me of strawberry ice cream," Nora whispered back.

"This way!" Aiden pushed through a gap in the bushes. "We've found it."

Through the bare branches, I caught sight of the ruined house. The crooked roof had gaps where tiles were missing and there was no glass at the windows. The snow dusting the rooftop made me think of icing sugar.

"It's the same place but do you really think Miss Mason's here?" Aiden muttered. "It doesn't look much like a House of Sweets."

My stomach lurched. I hoped we hadn't wasted our time coming up here. There were no lights, no voices and no sign of people. Annie was in terrible danger. At the very least she might be scared by now and missing home. If this was the wrong place I had to find out and get back to town.

Wingbeats shattered the air and a great bird

swooped down to the rooftop. Its beak gleamed in the moonlight, sharp as a knife.

"There! That's the bird I saw that night at Grimdean," I hissed.

"That's definitely an etting. I've seen pictures!" Nora gulped.

"I'm surprised the roof doesn't collapse under the weight of it – there's not many roof tiles left anyway," Aiden said.

I couldn't let some bird of death stop me. Pushing the branches out of my way, I got my sword ready and stepped into the clearing. Aiden had his bow poised. Nora stuffed the garlic butter in her pocket and the baguette under her jacket, and drew her torchblade.

"Try to keep out of sight of the windows." I skirted the edge of the clearing before darting to the corner of the house. From here I could see something blue on the doorstep. I jerked my head and the others followed, keeping low to avoid being seen.

When we reached the front door, my blood ran cold. A blue plate was piled high with gingerbread shapes – rabbits, hearts and stars. They smelt so tempting.

"No way!" Nora whispered behind me. "Miss Mason's not even trying to hide what she's doing."

The sweet smell of the gingerbread made my head swim. "It's there as a trap for anyone who tries to find her." I said. "One bite and you're enchanted."

I steeled myself to open the front door. There was no one inside. There were no sweets or cookies. There wasn't even any furniture, just rotten floorboards and dust. "I'm going in." The floor creaked as I stepped inside. Straight in front of me was a mouldy staircase leading to the upper floor.

Aiden followed me, his bow ready. "Creepy place!"

"Where are they?" My whisper stuck in my throat. "There's nothing here."

"I reckon you won't find anything without this." Nora picked up the blue plate. "It's an edible spell! Eat some gingerbread and then you'll see the House of Sweets. I've read about this kind of thing. Do you remember that book we looked at Robyn – *Enchantments and Illusions in the Unseen World*?"

I shook my head.

"Eating that is a bad idea! We'll forget things like Robyn's family did," Aiden said. "We might fall under the vampire's control."

"There's a way to stop the enchantment working fully," Nora said urgently. "You have to take a bite of the food and keep it in your mouth without swallowing."

I took a gingerbread rabbit off the plate. Its dark icing eye stared back at me, daring me to take a bite. Did I dare?

"Don't do it!" Aiden said.

"I have to do this to reach Annie. There's no other way!" The delicious smell of the gingerbread made my mouth water.

"I'll eat some too," Nora said.

"No, you guys have to stay here in case I get overcome by the enchantment," I said.

Aiden looked doubtful. "Are you sure you'll be able to bite some and not eat it?"

"I'm gonna try," I told him. "If I don't come out in ten minutes go back to Grimdean House and try to phone Miss Smiting."

The etting on the roof gave a loud cry. If that bird was waiting for someone to die I was probably walking into danger exactly the way it wanted.

I lifted the gingerbread rabbit to my lips and took a bite.

19

I Eat the Gingerbread

The gingerbread was the best thing I'd ever tasted but I knew I mustn't swallow it. I pushed the chunk into the side of my cheek. My pulse was doing a crazy rhythm all of its own. Was this going to work? It just had to. The information Nora passed on had never let us down before.

All at once, soft music tingled in the back of my mind. It was a sweet tune that sounded inviting. I held my breath and took a step forward.

Colour poured into the house like a movie come to life with me inside it. The walls glowed a perfect pink and the music grew stronger, but the thing that really knocked me out was the smell. Chocolate, strawberry, orange and a million other flavours of sweets washed through my brain. They were all here, somewhere, and I wanted them.

Aiden tapped me on the shoulder and jerked his thumb towards the door. His voice was muffled, but I understood. They were waiting for me outside. I needed to focus now. I'd come here for Annie and the other kids. I couldn't let them become part of Miss Mason's plan to make her wishes come true. A plan she'd kill for.

Laughter rang out from deeper inside and, as I turned towards the sound, pieces of the room filled in as if the place was being coloured by an invisible hand. Bright streamers hung along the walls and light poured down from a crystal chandelier. Pot plants sprung up in the corners. A table set for tea appeared in the centre of the room decorated with a vase of flowers.

A transparent boy about half my size brushed past me. I could see the wall behind him, like looking through dappled glass. "We're having something to eat," he told me. "I hope it's chocolate eclairs. They're my favourite."

It was Finlay – Aiden's next-door neighbour. I watched him grow more solid as he got closer to the table. I looked round, alert for any sign of Annie. There was a whisper in the corner and little footsteps on the stairs, but I couldn't hear her voice and I didn't dare call out for her. Miss Mason had to be here too and I wanted to stay out of her way for as long as possible.

A small, half-transparent hand slipped into mine. "Please could you sit with me?" said Finlay. "Then we can eat together."

"Sure," I whispered, sitting down beside him. "But where's everyone else?"

"I don't know." Finlay's gaze flicked up to the ceiling as he whispered, "I think they're still with *her*. She wants us to make wishes."

A creaking overhead made the hairs rise on the back of my neck. Was Miss Mason upstairs? Should I face her straight away or try to get the kids out first? I leant forwards. "What did she tell you to wish for?"

"She said we could wish for anything we liked!" A small girl with dark braids skipped to the chair opposite and sat down. "She said we were just getting started. I wished for these chocolate ladybirds." She opened her fingers. The little round sweets were already turning sticky in her hand. "Did you come for the party too?"

I played along. "Course I did! I love parties. But where's Annie?"

"Oh, she's here somewhere," the girl said. "She found some sherbet flowers upstairs."

"Sherbet flowers?" I couldn't help noticing the daydreamy look in the kids' eyes.

"Uh-huh, but they're not my favourite." The girl picked up her plate with both hands and bit into it.

I was so surprised I nearly swallowed the piece of gingerbread in my cheek. Then I realized the plate was actually a thin iced biscuit. The things on the table came into focus – chocolate drink mats, marshmallow cups and a bowl of marzipan fruit. Even the flowers were actually lollipops.

"I'm hungry." Finlay nibbled on his cup. "But I want to wait for the Grand Surprise!"

I frowned. This didn't sound good. "What's the Grand— no wait! It's a surprise, right? Who's bringing this surprise?"

Finlay and the girl with the braids leant forward and whispered to each other, before the girl replied, "The lady with the blonde hair and black eyes. She has a flute and when she plays it makes me feel tickly in my tummy – like I could do anything!"

I glanced round quickly, as if mentioning Miss Mason could make her appear. Whatever this surprise was, it couldn't be anything good. My heart started to race. I probably had very little time left to make my move.

Little footsteps tapped on the stairs.

"Annie?" I jumped up, knocking over my chair and breaking one of its biscuit legs.

A silver shadow of my sister ran to me, her hair swinging. "Robyn? You came to join in." She threw herself on to me. Her arms felt solid enough and her hair smelt of sherbet.

I choked up and struggled to get a grip on myself. "Annie, we're leaving. This is a bad place."

She let go of me and went to the table. "No, it's not! Anyway, I haven't tried everything yet."

"Yeah, we haven't tried everything." The girl with the braids pouted. "I want some white chocolate." She turned the vase upside down, pouring lollipops and a cascade of white chocolate stars on to the table.

"Is that all of you?" I said desperately. How was I going to persuade them all to leave?

"Don't forget him!" Annie pointed to the corner. I hadn't noticed the round-faced boy slumped in an armchair with a long, red shoelace sweet dangling from his mouth.

"There are four of you then." My brain spun. I

had to get them out of here without scaring them. "Hey, I've found something even better than these sweets. Do you want to see?"

"What is it?" The girl with the braids looked suspicious.

"Um. . ." What could it be? "It's a . . . it's a lemonade fountain with chocolate fishes and lily pads made of mint icing." I wondered if this sounded too crazy but their eyes lit up.

"I wanna see!" said the girl.

"Me too!" Annie said. "I wanna eat a chocolate fish!"

I plastered a smile on my face. "It's outside – I'll show you!"

There was a scraping noise upstairs, followed by heavy footsteps.

"Maybe we should wait for that lady's surprise," said the boy in the corner.

"Don't worry! We'll be back really quickly." I kept my smile bright. "Come on, it'll be fun!"

"Children!" called a honeyed voice. "Who are you talking to?"

I froze. Miss Mason spoke sweetly but there was a deadly cold note to her voice.

"It's Rob—" Annie began and I clapped a hand over her mouth.

"Don't tell her it's me!" I hissed. "Tell her you're talking to each other."

Annie nodded and for a moment the daydreamy look left her eyes. "We're talking to each other about the sweets!" she called back.

"How wonderful!" replied Miss Mason in the same sickly-sweet voice. "I'm sure you're all glad you came to my special party."

I clenched my fists. The evil monster! She was obviously planning to trick my sister and the others for as long as possible. Blood pounded in my ears. I longed to draw the frostblade and fight her but heavy footsteps on the stairs brought me to my senses. If I tried to attack the vampire right here and now the little kids could get hurt in the crossfire. I had to get them out safely first.

Seeing nowhere to hide, I slid under the table. The vampire's boots, all covered with rhinestones, came into focus on the wooden steps. "I think we should play our wishing game next, don't you?" Miss Mason said. "I know some really great things we could wish for!"

"What about the surprise?" Finlay asked.

"Oh, there's plenty of time for that!" Miss Mason reached the bottom of the stairs. I could just see the folds of her red velvet skirt through the legs of the table. "Here, have a little more gingerbread."

There was a moment of silence and I guessed the kids must be eating. An icy prickle ran across my skin. Cryptorum had warned us how powerful this vampire was and now I was close enough to touch her.

When the girl with the braids spoke again, her voice was slurred as if the gingerbread had fogged up her brain. "What shall we wish for, Miss Mason?"

"Where's that girl gone?" said the boy in the armchair. "She said there was a lemonade fountain."

"What girl?" Miss Mason snapped.

My blood ran cold. There was no time to get the kids out of here quietly. I had to tackle the vampire right now.

Drawing my blade, I leapt out from under the table. Miss Mason's blonde hair and red lips were as shiny as ever but her cheeks were covered by a river of dark veins. She gave a faint hiss as she saw me and for a second her sickly smile was replaced by a look of rage. Staring into her eyes was like gazing into two black holes. I had no doubt she wanted to kill me.

I gripped my sword tightly to stop my hand

shaking. "I know what you're doing. You're not going to touch any of them!"

"Robyn!" Annie tugged my sleeve.

I felt for her hand, keeping my eyes fixed on Miss Mason. "Annie, run out the front door! Now!"

Annie's chair scraped.

"Stay right where you are, Annie." The vampire's voice was smooth as treacle. "You don't want to miss all the sweets, do you?"

I felt Annie's hand fall out of my fingers. My little sister sank into her chair again. I dropped to my knees beside her. "Annie, come back with me." I looked into her daydreamy eyes and my heart went cold. How was I going to fight an enchantment this strong?

"Miss . . . the . . . sweets," Annie mumbled.

My little sister was lost again.

Feeling a lump in my throat, I started to swallow. The chunk of gingerbread! I'd nearly eaten it. I pushed it to the side of my cheek. It was soggy now and I could feel it falling to mush in my mouth.

Miss Mason watched me closely. "So you've figured out a way to see through the enchantment without falling under its spell. You think you're pretty clever don't you?"

"Not really." I stepped back as she came closer, and she laughed.

"Once I heard that Erasmus Cryptorum had repaired the Mortal Clock, I planned my return to Wendleton and my disguise," she continued. "I was sure I could get inside Grimdean and discover what the old man was up to. Then I found you fresh, young Chimes and I knew destroying you would be my first step in getting revenge. So I'm delighted you've come here tonight." She smiled like a wolf.

The room flickered to grey and back to colour as the gingerbread fell apart in my mouth. I told myself not to swallow.

"Time's up, Chime girl! Now all you get to do is watch from the outside." Miss Mason's icy hand gripped my throat. Her fingernails felt like claws digging into my skin.

I tried to swing my blade but she thrust me backwards, my feet skidding on the wooden floor. Her fingers tightened round my neck until she gave me one final shove and I fell through the doorway on to the cold ground outside.

I spat out the last crumbs of the gingerbread just as the front door slammed. The snow had stopped falling but the thin covering on the ground soaked right through my clothes. The moon came out, casting a ghostly gleam across the white landscape.

"Robyn!" Nora was at my side. "Are you OK? Did you find the kids?"

My neck throbbed painfully. "There are four of them," I croaked. "Where's the gingerbread? I'm going back in."

Aiden took a gingerbread mouse and snapped it into three pieces. "We're all going in. One piece each. Ready?"

We each put a piece in our mouth. After a moment the House of Sweets filled in again like a beautiful picture, with sparkling windows and a polished wooden door. Music began to play – a flute with notes so enchanting they made me ache inside. As the music stopped, a glistening framework like pink icing sprouted from the ground all along the walls, forming a cage across every wall, window and door.

I grabbed hold of the weird pink mesh. It was so cold it burned into my hand and I let go again. "Geez, what is that?"

"Something to keep the kids inside and us out here," Aiden said grimly.

I leant as close to the window as I could without touching the mesh. Miss Mason was circling the kids' chairs, a hungry look in her eyes. As her skin grew paler, the black veins on her face darkened. Already three bright wish bubbles floated in the air.

"But I can't wish any harder!" whined Finlay.

"Of course you can," Miss Mason said sweetly. "And when you get it right you'll get the Grand Surprise. You want that don't you? Now say it again and you have to mean it this time."

Finlay gulped. "I wish Pearl was inde . . . indestruct-ible."

We Face a Swarm of Deadly Creatures

oozy from the enchanted gingerbread, the kids inside the House of Sweets repeated Miss Mason's words, bringing to life one terrible wish after another.

"I wish Pearl had super-strength," piped Annie.

"I wish Pearl had the power to read minds," said Finlay.

"I wish that Mr Cryptorum would vanish for ever," repeated the girl with the braids. A look of horror passed over her face as if she'd realized what a terrible thing she'd said. Then her face went blank again.

A crowd of gleaming wishes hovered above the table. Each one had a smoky-grey surface but the picture inside was clear and sharp. They looked perfect – and deadly. If these came true then Wendleton and everyone in it could be wiped out by Miss Mason's revenge.

"Annie, stop!" I rattled the mesh, ignoring the burning cold. "Don't say any more of her wishes!"

"Robyn!" Annie twisted to face me, jolted from her daydream. The wish she'd just made about Pearl's super-strength popped in a shower of colour.

Miss Mason flashed me a look of pure hatred. "Annie, dear!" she said silkily. "I want to talk to you. Tell me: is your sister always nice to you?"

"I . . . um." Annie faltered.

"Sisters aren't always nice, are they?" The vampire smiled sweetly. "But *I'll* be good to you and I'll give you every kind of sweet you can think of."

Had I been nice to Annie? I couldn't help thinking of all the times I'd wanted her to go away – all the times I hadn't listened to her recorder playing, the times I'd told her to stop bothering me. . .

"Have some more gingerbread!" The vampire thrust another piece into my little sister's mouth. "You don't need a sister when you have me."

I rattled the mesh but Annie didn't turn this time. What was I going to do now?

Nora had found a long stick, stuck it through the cage and wedged the letter box open. Aiden crouched down and fired a silver arrow through the narrow slot, but it missed. "I can't shoot any closer! She's standing too near the kids."

Stepping back, I swung at the mesh with my frostblade but the sword bounced off with a loud clang. "Annie!" I shouted. "Think of your real wishes. Remember how you wished to be a unicorn!"

Annie didn't move.

"Now there's one more wish you're going to make!" Miss Mason hissed. "All of you say it after me: *I wish that everyone born on the stroke of midnight would die.*"

The kids repeated the words in robot-like voices. Four identical wishes floated out of their mouths. Pearl Mason's hand moved and I saw the knife hidden in the folds of her skirt. For these wishes to come true, they had to be the last ones the kids would ever make.

"Annie!" I screamed.

Annie coughed and the gingerbread piece came out of her mouth. Jumping up, she dashed to the door and flung it open, shattering the weird pink mesh. Then she ran straight into my arms.

"Annie, stay behind me!" I told her. "Miss Mason is dangerous!" Annie clung to me even tighter.

Miss Mason followed Annie outside, the dark veins spreading down her neck and arms like a deadly black river. She smiled and frost-white fangs grew in her mouth. This was Miss Mason as she really was – the vampire Pearl.

"Fire arrows!" Aiden yelled, shooting off a volley.

I pushed Annie behind me, fitted an arrow to my bow and fired. Only one arrow found its target. Smiling, Pearl yanked it from her shoulder and threw it to the ground. Then she pursed her lips and blew a deafening whistle.

The undergrowth rustled. Snow tumbled off the swaying branches. Like a spiny tidal wave, the kobolds swept out of the shadows. Behind them, an army of bony white figures sprang into the clearing, clicking as they ran.

"Scree sags!" I shouted.

Annie screamed and ran back into the house, and Aiden raced after her calling to the kids to block the door. Nora turned her arrows on the kobolds, knocking them down one by one. A cloud of bats flew over the clearing. Gathering into a swarm, they swooped on the kobolds, with three or four attacking each one.

Pearl sprang at me and I parried. My frostblade met her knife, stopping the blow. She twisted sideways and I felt my jacket rip under her blade.

I pushed her away and took another swing. This time she dived in low. The blade missed my legs but caught me off balance and I went down. Two scree sags jumped on me, their bony fingers clutching at my jacket. Aiden charged them, his sword crunching into white ribs, and they collapsed into a pile of bones. Aiden grabbed my arm and pulled me up.

"Thanks!" I gasped.

"Sure!" He spun round and charged the next group of scree sags.

I faced Pearl again. A nasty smile played on her lips as she swung at me. "You – will – not – win, Robyn Silver!" She aimed a knife blow with every word.

Tearing the frostblade from my hands, she grabbed hold of me. Her fangs were close to my throat.

"Robyn, here!" Nora ripped off the cellophane and threw me the garlic baguette.

Catching it, I thrust the baguette at Pearl's fangs. Shrieking, she fell back. The smell of the garlic was overwhelming. Then Nora lobbed the lump of garlic butter, which hit the vampire round the head with a satisfying *thunk*.

That gave me enough time to grab the frostblade. I faced the vampire with my sword in one hand and a garlic baguette in the other.

Snarling, Pearl leapt at me. Smashing the baguette out of my hand, her claw-like fingers reached for my throat. Her hands felt like ice. We struggled and I pushed her off, but she leapt at me again.

Time seemed to freeze. I fumbled, trying to block her knife blow. Then she tripped over a kobold and fell right on top of my blade. For a terrible moment, her hands reached out for me. Then she crumbled, burning away until there was nothing left but a pile of ash on the snow. A knife with a razor-sharp point lay beside it.

I stumbled backwards, the swirly markings glowing on my blade. The sword must have struck her heart. Then I'd won? A feeling of relief rushed over me, followed by a massive pile of kobolds, their spines scraping my skin.

A torchblade swung through the air and the kobolds scattered. "Nora!" I scrambled up. "Pretty nice moves!"

"Thanks!" she grinned and together we ran towards the House of Sweets.

Aiden was fighting scree sags, his blade crunching into them one after another, but he was outnumbered and they were driving him backwards.

"Aiden, come on!" I yelled. "Get inside the house!"

A wave of kobolds and scree sags chased after us, biting and gnashing. We slammed the door and leant against it. Aiden clutched at a long jagged cut on his arm. Annie and the other kids stared at us as if they'd just woken from a dream. The table and the sweets were fading and Pearl's wishes were gone completely.

"How are we going to get them out of here?" Aiden muttered. "There are too many monsters."

A terrible high-pitched cry went up from a cluster of scree sags gathered round the vampire's ashes and this seemed to shake up the rest of the creatures. Some of the kobolds ran back into the trees and others started attacking each other. The scree sags ran at the house, drumming on the door and windows with their bony fingers.

"I want to go home!" squeaked the girl with the braids, bursting into tears.

"I'll go out there and draw them away from the house," I said to Aiden and Nora. "Then you can get the kids back to town."

"No!" Aiden glared at me, still clutching his bleeding arm. "Better if we fight together."

"You can't though, can you? You're hurt!" I said.

"Robyn, you can't do this on your own!" Nora cried.

"It's the only way!" I took Annie's hand. "Listen, all of you! Aiden and Nora are going to take you home so be good and do as they say. I'll catch up with you soon."

"I want the lemonade fountain with the chocolate fishes," said the boy in the armchair. "I can't see any of the sweets any more."

"Nor can I!" said Annie.

I realized I'd probably swallowed the gingerbread sometime during the fight but with Miss Mason gone the enchantment must have lifted.

"When we get back I'll buy you mountains of sweets," Nora promised.

I hugged my sister. Her little arms fastened round my neck and I had to pull away. The bashing on the windows was growing louder. Snarling white faces leant right up to the glass.

I grabbed the door knob. "Barricade it behind me until you know it's safe," I told Aiden. Then I unsheathed my sword and flung the door open, sending a few scree sags flying. Sweeping my blade in a wide arc, I leapt to the centre of the clearing.

"Hey, monsters!" I yelled. "Come and get me!" Not the greatest line but it was the only one I could think of. Then I sprinted past the house into a patch of trees. I had to get deeper into the heathland and draw the monsters after me, leaving the way clear for Nora, Aiden and the kids to escape.

I ran fast. I had no idea what lay ahead but I didn't dare slow down. I looked back just as the moon came out from behind a cloud. A heaving mass of kobolds and scree sags were chasing me.

I gulped. My plan was working!

After a few minutes, I came to the network of ditches and pools that we'd stumbled into last time. A picture of the water monsters we'd seen popped into my head – the vodanoys with their grey slimy skin and webbed hands, and the nesha, the closest thing the Unseen World had to a deadly octopus. But there was no way to turn back so I jumped over the ditches, dodging the worst bits of swamp as best I could.

When I glanced back again, the kobolds had stopped at the swamp edge. Their stubby legs weren't long enough to let them jump the ditches. The scree sags were still coming at me though. As

I watched, a pale tentacle rose from the marsh and took one down.

I was starting to think I might make it to the other side before them, when I saw the etting. The great black bird swooped overhead, calling sharply. Obviously it had got tired of waiting for me to die and had come to finish me off.

I was so busy trying to duck as it dived at me that I nearly ran straight off a cliff. For a moment I swayed over the drop, before grabbing a branch to pull myself backwards. A fierce icy wind whirled around me. Fumbling for my torch, I shone the light at the rock face. There was no safe way down. Except ... there were some footholds and handholds just below where I was standing and if I could fool the scree sags for long enough I might just beat them.

Switching off the torch, I turned to face them, sword ready.

They slowed down when they saw the frostblade. Making a semicircle, they advanced on me, their faces grinning and bones clicking.

I waited till the very last second. Bony fingers brushed my throat and with a yell I swung myself down the cliff. The scree sags gave their high-pitched cry and threw themselves after me. They fell, one by one and more scree sags piled after them. Cracking sounds filled the air as they smacked into the ground below.

I was climbing by feel alone and I lost my foothold a couple of times. The cliff was cold and slippery with snow, but I held on. When I was sure the scree sags were gone, I pulled myself to the top and staggered back across the marsh. My legs felt like jelly.

Something swooped overhead and I ducked, expecting the etting, but the engine roar and the lights meant this was no monster. The helicopter landed in the clearing on the other side of the house.

I had a sinking feeling. I was pretty sure I knew who I was going to see. As I rounded the corner of the house, three lean figures in black leather leapt out of the helicopter. With a swish of their ultrasonic blades, they rounded up two sleeping kobolds from under a log and a scree sag with a limp. They had them all tied up in meta-tensile rope before I could say Beast Undercover Tracking Taskforce.

"Hi, Robyn." Rufus knotted the rope around the dozy kobolds. "We were passing by and we noticed all the monster activity on our subthermal scanner. Looks like you got pretty beat up."

Portia put away her sword and smoothed her hair into place. "Seems like we saved you. Good thing we stopped by."

It took a massive effort not to roll my eyes. "Shame you weren't here an hour ago to help defeat a vampire and her army, but I guess your Mr Dray couldn't be bothered with anything so small." I glanced into the helicopter. Obviously Mr Dray had stayed safely at home.

"Yeah, right!" Portia sneered. "Like you could defeat a vampire."

"I didn't do it alone – Nora and Aiden were here."

"You reckon we're going to believe that?" Tristan said.

"I don't care whether you believe it. I just want to use your helicopter." I marched past them and climbed on board. "Well, are you coming or not?"

Annie and Me
Take Our First
Helicopter Ride

told the helicopter pilot to follow the road down from the snowy heath. We found Aiden, Nora and the kids just outside of town. The kids were falling over with tiredness. Nora was holding hands with Annie and the girl with the braids, while Aiden was giving Finlay a piggyback. The other little boy, who still had a red shoelace sweet dangling from his mouth, had sat down on the icy path and was refusing to go any further.

We landed in the next-door field and I yelled to Aiden to bring the kids over.

"We can't have this many people on board," Rufus told me as I put the kids on the helicopter. "You'll overload it."

"These kids can't walk any more," I said. "So I guess some of us Chimes will have to walk instead." I held his gaze until he looked away.

"What! I'm not walking just because they decided to bring kids up here," Portia said.

Finlay burst into tears and after a minute of wailing Portia got off, muttering about the horrible noise. Rufus climbed down too. Tristan stayed in the corner with a stubborn look on his face. I made Aiden get on. He didn't say anything but I could see from his face that the wound on his arm really hurt.

"You should go!" Nora brushed off my attempt to get her on board. "Annie will feel better if you're with her and someone has to show these guys the way."

"OK, thanks! Meet us at Grimdean House," I yelled as we took off again.

The helicopter soared over town. I held tight to my sister and I was pretty glad when we landed on the Grimdean lawn. Lights were on inside the house. Snow began falling thickly as Mr Cryptorum came marching down the garden.

"What on earth do you think you're doing landing here at this time of night?" he barked at the pilot before spotting me inside. "Robyn!

What's going on?"

By the time we'd got the kids inside and Miss Smiting had treated Aiden's arm, I'd told Cryptorum all about the gingerbread enchantment and how we'd guessed the location of Miss Mason's lair. Cryptorum's expression grew scarily fierce at my description of the House of Sweets and how the vampire had forced the children to make her wishes. When I'd finished, he took us to the kitchen and made everyone jam sandwiches and mugs of warm milk.

"You did well to find Pearl. It was a wild guess but instinct is what makes a good Chime," Cryptorum said at last. "Miss Smiting and I found a group of vampires in the farmhouse hideout. They were easily beaten but there was no sign of Pearl herself. We knew something was wrong when the bats came to find us and we returned straight away. Dominic Dray's reports about Pearl must have been mistaken."

It took me a moment to remember he was talking about Miss Mason. I couldn't get used to calling her Pearl. I glanced at Tristan, who was sullenly sipping his drink. I had forgotten the information taking Cryptorum out of town had come from Dominic Dray.

Cryptorum shook his head. "When I think how close Pearl got to making herself invincible... I should have destroyed that *Wishes and Mysteries* book long ago."

I shuffled in my seat. He hadn't told me off for taking the book out of his study without asking but I felt pretty guilty anyway.

"We musst worry about that tomorrow," Miss Smiting put in. "For now we need to get these children home."

"Why are we here?" piped up the girl with the braids. "What happened to the place with all the sweets?"

"The lemon sherbet was awesome!" Annie's eyes lit up then her happy smile wavered. "But Miss Mason wasn't as nice as before. Her eyes were really scary!"

I put my arm round her. I wanted to say that none of it had been real but I couldn't bring myself to lie. "You don't need to worry about it. Everything's fine now."

Tristan took out a small pyramid of polished bronze and flicked a button on the base. A green spark began dancing on its tip. "Give them a shock with this Cranial Neutralizer. That'll zap their memory of the whole thing."

"Put that away, boy!" Cryptorum barked, making us all jump. "I've seen people forget years of their lives after using one of those. A rose quartz crystal is the proper way to treat shock. I've been relying on it for forty years."

Annie and the others gazed into Cryptorum's big pink crystal, which made their memories of the night fade and let them forget how scared they'd been. Then Miss Smiting drove us all home.

When I knocked on our door, Sammie opened it wearing pyjamas. "Do you KNOW what time it is?"

"Yeah, sorry." I pulled Annie inside before she could close the door on us.

"I'm telling Mum in the morning," Sammie said fiercely. "You're going to be in so much trouble tomorrow."

I led Annie upstairs and she climbed straight into bed fully dressed.

"There was a party, wasn't there? That's what I remember. And then we ended up going to Grimdean House in a helicopter." Her little forehead wrinkled as she yawned. "Was it a party, Robyn?"

I went to the window. The snow was falling thickly like a moving white curtain. I was glad Annie was safe inside with me. I tucked the blanket round her and switched off the light. "Let's talk about it in the morning."

"I remember a big house and lots and lots of sweets." Her words started to slur with sleepiness. "It was mostly good. Except . . . I don't think wishes should be something scary. Do you, Robyn?"

In the morning snow lay deeply everywhere and the bright sunshine made it gleam like the icing on top of a Christmas cake. "Make sure you all put hats, gloves and boots on today. It's cold out there." Mum set another juice carton down on the breakfast table. Three pairs of hands reached for it but Ben got there first. "Were you at Aiden's yesterday, Robyn? I fell asleep on the sofa and had a very strange dream – something about gingerbread."

I hid a smile. Obviously things were too hazy for her to get really cross with me.

Dad rustled the newspaper and cut in before I could reply. "More bad news about the Ashbrook School building," he said to my mum. "They've just discovered damage to the foundations. It's going to take them months to fix it – maybe a year."

"They won't get much repair work done in this snow," Mum said. "Mrs Lovell must be desperate –

stuck in that big old house and trying to keep that grouchy old man happy."

"Mr Cryptorum's not that bad!" I said.

Sammie stared at me. "Just because he runs that stupid Bat Club. What's so great about bats anyway?"

"They're the only mammal that can fly," I said, helping myself to extra jam. That shut Sammie up for a minute. She didn't know I'd learnt the fact from Nora.

"What are they going to do, though?" Mum said. "Josh, eat up please. I mean, Mr Cryptorum isn't going to want the school in his house for ever. People are saying it was his assistant who arranged it anyway."

Dad shook his head and turned the page. For a moment I wanted to tell them the real reason we'd moved to Grimdean House: how Miss Smiting had decided that Cryptorum needed more Chimes and that's how it had all begun. But they wouldn't understand. They couldn't even see my Chime world.

I sighed. "I'd better get to school."

"Yeah, go and find your Bat Club friends," Sammie said. "I'm sure *they'll* be happy to see you."

I stopped in the doorway and looked back. Mum was spreading jam on Annie's toast, while Josh and Annie kicked each other under the table. Dad was turning the pages of his newspaper, Ben was pouring more juice and Sammie was tapping out the rhythm to a pop song.

I turned to go. I hadn't admitted it to myself till now but I'd started to feel like I didn't belong with them any more. There was a whole world I was part of that my family would never see. So how could they really know me at all? It was like there was an invisible wall between me and them.

A little hand slipped into mine. "You were there in my dream." Annie frowned like she was trying to figure something out. "You wanted me to be safe and you knew what to do. You always know what to do."

I stopped in surprise. "Of course I want you to be safe. You're my sister."

Annie hugged me. "Can you read to me tonight?" She dropped her voice to a whisper. "And we can have a midnight feast!"

I laughed. "All right then! As long as it's a midnight feast with crisps. I'm sick of sweets."

She grinned at me. I felt a bit better as I went to find my gloves and hat. I guess some things had changed in the last few weeks and one of those things was me, but that was just the way it went sometimes.

Cryptorum Tells Me a Secret

The helicopter had disappeared from the Grimdean lawn that morning. It felt strange that all the kids and teachers carried on as if nothing had happened. Everyone was excited about the snow – especially the little kids – but the deadly vampire whose wishes could've killed everyone might as well have never existed.

By the end of lessons there was a silver Rolls-Royce parked next to the limo out front. An expensive-looking black coat hung from the coat stand in the hallway. I was pretty sure it was Mr Dray's.

"Robyn!" Nora came running down the passage. "The BUTT kids are here. Aiden's fighting Rufus –

torchblade against ultrasonic!"

"Who's winning?" I sped after her.

The door to the bat barn was open and Cryptorum was outlined in the doorway. At the far end of the lawn, two figures were circling each other in the snowy twilight. Tristan and Portia were standing to the side, cheering every move Rufus made whether it was any good or not.

"Aiden agreed to fight after Rufus dared him," Nora muttered to me. "Rufus went on and on about how Aiden's improved blade could never match proper technological advances."

Both boys were in protective leather jackets and the expressions on their faces were deadly serious. At a year older and at least five inches taller, Rufus was getting in a lot more hits. I found myself wishing Rufus had dared me, and then I felt bad for doubting Aiden's fighting skills.

"Robyn?" Cryptorum was right behind me. I hadn't heard him come over. "Go up to my study, please. There's a ball of twine on my desk that I need."

"But, sir! I don't want to miss this." I kept my gaze fixed on the fight.

Rufus swung his ultrasonic blade catching Aiden on the shoulder. Aiden dodged away and thrust under the older boy's guard. The blow caught him on the stomach.

"Foul!" Portia cried. "That hit was too low."

"It was not!" I yelled.

"Robyn!" Cryptorum's tone was stern.

Reluctantly I dragged myself back to the house and ran upstairs to the north wing. Bursting into Cryptorum's study, I went straight to his desk. If I was quick I might still catch the end of the fight.

I stopped short.

Dominic Dray was sitting in Cryptorum's chair, his black hair perfectly combed. He was wearing an expensive-looking black suit and purple tie like something out of a clothes catalogue. His silver-topped walking stick rested against the side of the desk. He was examining a photo in a frame. It was the one of Cryptorum, his wife and Miss Smiting. Placing it back on the desk, he smiled at me. "Miss Silver, how fortuitous that you should arrive. Are you looking for me?"

"No, for this." I picked up a coil of green wire. I guessed it must be what Cryptorum wanted. I glanced through the window behind Dray. The fir trees at the end of the garden were fading into the dark and the bats were starting to circle.

"And how did you enjoy my helicopter last

night?" Dray studied me, his hands clasped neatly together. "It was much preferable to trekking all the way home on foot I'm sure."

"It was great – thanks." I looked away. There was something about him that made me uneasy.

"And the other advantages we have – the scanners and the ultrasonic blades – I'm sure you can see the benefit of these things. Perhaps you wish you had them too."

I frowned. "Rufus is fighting Aiden with an ultrasonic blade right now and he hasn't won yet."

Dray waved his hand dismissively. "It's not just the blades! We have a state-of-the-art training facility in the grounds of Kesterly Manor. There are environmental controls in the combat studio which create rain, snow, heat – whatever conditions you need to train in. We have an underground bunker with a full-sized town mocked up inside." He grasped his cane, stood up and came round the desk to meet me. His voice softened. "Can you imagine how wonderful it would be to train at Kesterly? I would like you to join us and become one of the best."

I hesitated. "You're really asking me to join?" For a moment I pictured myself in a combat studio with every kind of equipment inside. I'd never seen the place, but in my imagination it looked pretty great. "But didn't you train Rufus and the others from when they were little? I've only just started."

"That will not be a problem," Dray said. "You already have potential and I think you would benefit greatly from what Kesterly can offer. Shall I tell Mr Cryptorum that you are moving to further your training?"

The image in my head burst like a throwaway wish. "It sounds nice, but I can't," I said flatly. "My friends are here. My family's here. I can't just leave."

"I understand it would be difficult." Dray's blue eyes glinted. "But what if we could explain it all to them nicely? Give you a scholarship to my school, perhaps?"

"I'm sorry. I just don't think it would work."

Dray stepped towards the window, leaning on his cane. "So you would put all your faith and Wendleton's future into the hands of a man who hasn't told you any of his secrets?" He turned to look at me. "Where does he keep the caged wish these days?"

I didn't reply. I was so surprised that I glanced at the white cupboard on the wall without meaning to.

Dray smiled. It wasn't a nice smile this time.

Taking the twine from my hand, he advanced on the cupboard. Shimmying the end of the wire in the padlock, he had the door open in less than a minute. The wish tumbled over and over inside the glass case. It had a beautiful green sheen on its surface but I'd seen beautiful things that were deadly before. I still couldn't make out the picture inside it.

"I don't—" I broke off. I'd been about to say I didn't care what the secret wish was but the truth was I did want to know. "It's none of our business."

"What if it's something that would endanger people's lives if it ever got loose?" Dray said. "Because I *guarantee* you it would."

My stomach lurched. Was the wish dangerous? I didn't want to believe him but he sounded pretty sure. "Even if that's true it's still not going to persuade me to go to Kesterly Manor. Those kids you're training think they're better than everyone else." I kept my eyes fixed on him in case he tried to free the wish. If it was dangerous like he said, it was best off in its case.

It was strange how everyone who came in here wanted to see it – first Miss Mason with her shadow and now Mr Dray – and yet only people close to Cryptorum were supposed to know it existed. The whole thing was odd . . . but maybe that was it! That was the connection!

The pieces started slotting together in my head. "Miss Mason – I mean Pearl – knew about this wish. The first time I saw her shadow-walking she was looking for it. It was you that told her, wasn't it?" I stared at him. "That's how she knew. That's probably when she became fixed on learning about the power of final wishes. And you told Mr Cryptorum that you'd found her lair in an empty farmhouse and that's why he left town. It all makes sense. She never would have known about the last wish without you!"

"How *dare* you accuse me of colluding with a vampire!" He pointed his cane at me. "You should remember who you're talking to! I am not used to listening to this sort of nonsense."

But I couldn't stop myself now. My pulse was racing. "You probably wanted the vampire to free this wish because you don't like Mr Cryptorum. My little sister was one of the ones taken away by the vampire. Did you know that?"

Dray jabbed his cane at me. "You have absolutely no proof that I had anything to do with it. You've made a disastrous choice not to join us at Kesterly and I will make sure you regret it for a long, long time."

The study door opened and Cryptorum stood framed in the doorway. "It is *her* choice though, Dominic. If she doesn't want to train at Kesterly there's nothing else to be said. And what's this talk of proof about?"

"I think he told the vampire about the wish in your cupboard," I burst out. "I think he's been tricking us all along."

Dray's face darkened. "This is slander! Erasmus, we've been friends for forty years but if you cannot control your Chime pupils I shall not be coming back here."

"Friends are we?" Cryptorum's craggy eyebrows lowered. "I'm not saying she's right but friends help each other out when trouble comes and that's not what you've done for me the past few days."

"I thought you'd be able to handle one vampire in your own town!" Dray sneered. "Clearly I was wrong."

The two men glared at each other and for a second I thought Cryptorum would pull out his frostblade. "You'd better go, Dominic, before I lose my temper," he said at last. "I'll take you to your car."

"I'll see myself out, thank you!" Dray said icily, pushing past the other man and heading for the stairs.

When he'd left, Mr Cryptorum paced up and down. Eye crept out from under the desk but quickly scuttled back into hiding again. "You may be right about what he did," Cryptorum said at last. "I didn't want to believe that Dominic would betray me – we've known each other for such a long time."

I clenched my hands. "If he told Miss Mason to come here then he's not a true Chime!"

"I know." Cryptorum walked to the window.

I picked the twine off the floor, where Mr Dray had dropped it. "He really wanted me to go to Kesterly Manor. He wanted me to train there."

"I thought he might ask you. I wanted you to have the choice."

"I didn't ask for one," I muttered. Did he want to get rid of me or something?

"Come here, I want to show you something." Cryptorum went to the cupboard with the wish. He placed his hand against the case and the wish pressed itself against the same spot on the other side of the glass. "Many years ago, my wife Rebecca was wounded by Pearl. This was her last wish before she died and, as you know, last wishes can be very powerful. I can't allow this one to go free in case it comes true."

"Is it . . . dangerous?"

Cryptorum sighed. "It could be. You see, Rebecca saw how much of a burden my Chime duties were. She saw how hard it was always to be fighting the next monster that no one else can see. So with her last breath she wished that I could be free of it all – free of my Chime powers."

"But that's not a bad wish."

"No, it isn't. But I couldn't give it the chance to come true. Who would fight if I didn't? Who would protect people? I felt I had a duty." Cryptorum paused.

I leaned in to look more closely at the wish. I could see the picture inside now. It was Cryptorum as he would have been without Chime powers. He looked younger, happier, and his eyebrows were definitely less scary. The clock outside struck the hour with deep, slow chimes. Cryptorum took his hand off the glass and the wish floated away again.

"Your fighting skills are strong," Cryptorum went on. "That's why Dominic Dray wants you. He must have discovered from his students that you were the one that killed Pearl. You may find a lot rests on you in the future but at least you have something I didn't."

"What's that?"

"Friends who have Chime powers too. I think you're going to need them."

I didn't have the chance to say any more because Nora raced in followed by Aiden. "Guess what?" Nora's freckled face was pink. "Aiden beat Rufus with the torchblade and then Rufus went off in a huff!"

"Nice one!" I said.

"Basically, I kicked some BUTT!" Aiden grinned. "You shoulda seen his face."

"He's a bad loser," Nora agreed.

I followed the others out of the door but Cryptorum called me back. "Robyn?" His mouth twitched at the corners.

I swung round. "Yes, sir?"

"You did well on Blagdurn Heath. But don't ever, *ever* borrow my best sword again."

"Yes, sir."

Aiden gave me a blow by blow report of his fight with Rufus as we ran out of Grimdean House. Nora interrupted with extra bits here and there.

"Rufus is a show off!" I said, closing the front door. "I just wish—" Then I stopped myself. It was wishing that'd caused all the problems in the first place. Maybe the world was better off without them.

Nora glanced at me as if she understood. "I wish

he'd stop being such a dork," she said. "And I wish they'd cook Friday lunchtime food every day of the week." The wishes popped out of her mouth and drifted into the air.

We trekked down the snowy street. Christmas lights twinkled in the shop windows and carols drifted out of Lipson's.

Aiden joined in. "I wish I was having hot dogs for dinner with extra fries." His wishes floated up to join Nora's. They were round and shiny in the dim light.

My spirits lifted. They were just wishes – little bubbles of hope that couldn't hurt anyone. "Hey, think bigger!" I said. "I wish the Christmas holidays would come early. I wish the bats would raid the shops in town and bring us cake. I wish Lovell would dance the tango in our next assembly!"

My wishes went spinning up to join the others. Then a gust of wind caught them all and took them away, soaring over Grimdean House into the darkening sky.

KOBOLD

KOBOLD

Small but extremely vicious – they look like a spiky goblin crossed with a bad-tempered porcupine. Approach at your own peril – those teeth are sharp.

VODANOY

VODANOY

These sneaky cousins of kobolds like to rear up out of lakes, ditches and ponds and attack. Their grey skin is raised in ridges along their body and they have large webbed hands and feet – all the better for dragging people under the water...

BOGGUN

BOGGUN

Often found lurking in dark corners, feeding off any sadness or fear in the room. You'll likely see a silhouetted shape out of the corner of your eye – but if you look straight at them, they vanish ... and reappear just behind you!

SCREE SAG

SCREE SAG

These skeleton-like creatures have bodies made of bare bones, with small dark eyes and bloodless lips. Their long fingers are designed for throttling their prey – and they pretend to be a non-threatening pile of bones before animating and attacking.

ETTING

ETTING

These malicious black birds
hover over creatures who are
close to death, in the nasty
hope of feeding off their
departing souls. Beware their
large, sharp beaks.

GRODDER

GRODDER

Not the most intelligent of
otherworldly monsters, these
enormous, hairy bull-like creatures
use brute force when attacking.
If you're unlucky enough to
spot their dangerous horns and
fiery red eyes, there's only
one thing to do – RUN!

NESHA

NESHA

A terrifying underwater denizen with 12 huge tentacles – these have suckers attached to ensnare their prey. Try not to faint when you spot their six angry eyes and mouth full of spiky teeth – you'll be dragged down into the deep before you know it.

(

Paula Harrison is a best-selling children's author, with worldwide sales of over one million copies. Her books include *The Rescue Princesses* series. She wanted to be a writer from a young age but spent many happy years being a primary school teacher first.

Follow Paula on Twitter **@P_Harrison99** or visit her website **www.paulaharrison.jimdo.com**